Humble Task

CATHLEEN ELLIS

Cover design by Launie Parry
Interior design by Veronica Yager

ISBN: 978-1629671185
Library of Congress Control Number: 2018902074

Other Books by Cathleen Ellis

www.CathleenEllis.com

A Scarf of Promise

Castle in the Air

Making Our Way

Kara's Love

Baskets on Christmas Lane

Up To Me

Christmas Bright

A Voice for Gabby

Love Ties

Roses for Meredith

Old Crooked Road

Just Let It Go

Tend My Flowers

Together Now

Sky Tossed

1

Summer 2006

"Baby, I'm so glad to be out tonight, goin' to a movie with you."

He touched her cheek as they sat together at the ice cream shop.

Julie stared at Jace. He watched her shake her head as tears began to stream down her cheeks.

"In two days, just two, she'll be gone. Dad's taking us to Granddad Thurston's," she breathed in and blew out a breath, "tomorrow. It's a blast at his ranch, riding horses, helping with chores, puttin' up the hay, helping Grandma with the cookin'."

"You're kidding me, pickin' up poop, muckin' the stalls, come on, Julie."

She watched him give her his look, rolling his eyes. He ruffled her honey-colored hair and gave her a big smile. But inside, Jace tasted vomit rising up into his throat. He took a big gulp from his water glass, to ease the puke down.

They held hands, in the quiet of their booth, hearing chattering noise around them. Jace's thoughts raced back to one week ago this night. Julie told him. Cheri, her mom, planned to leave the family home and relocate down to Baker City, near Lake Mead. She would go alone. She completed her Certified Nursing Assistant (CNA) training.

Then Cheri worked a night shift at a senior living facility near their home in Empireville, Nevada. Julie took over running the Thurston home while her mom slept during the day. Little did Julie know that it was in preparation for her mom's departure.

He felt Julie's fingers pressing against his. He turned, smiled to her and kissed her cheek.

"Sorry, I was somewhere else."

"Yeah, I know, I go back to my thoughts some. But lately, Jace," she paused and looked him square in the face, "I been doin' a whole lot of praying. Our family's gotta go on. Dad loves his job in the casino, cage manager, works 12 hour shifts, 10 to 10 p.m. We see him on Thursdays, his day off, been that way since, like forever, it seems."

"It's part of the occupational hazard," he stopped and shook his head, "of all people who work in the gaming industry, the long shifts, crazy days off."

"Uh huh, just like folks in the health professions, same deal."

"You guys just haven't lived a regular 9-5 Monday to Friday kind of life. Are you ready?"

"Yup," she paused, "I gotta go, take me home, then, I gotta face everything. Jace, my anger just consumes me sometimes, her pullin' a stunt like this. It all falls on me. And my siblings, they fight like crazy, one of them's gonna get hurt. I sure as heck can't handle those two."

He saw her brightly lit eyes, angry brown now.

As he left her at her doorstep, his lips sought hers, a soft caress.

"God loves you, Julie, and so do I."

"I'll be thinkin' about you while I'm at the ranch."

"And you'll be in my thoughts, Jules, as I sit at the pool. Never realized when I got my WSI that being a lifeguard would be so boring."

"See ya."

They hugged, and Julie walked into her home.

ℰ⅁

"Granddad Thurston, you see how bad it is between them."

"Uh huh, I see it now. I'll keep Derek here another week, try to talk some sense into him. Amy'll go back with you; school's starting soon. I gotta head out for a meeting in town."

Julie went to her granddad for a hug. Later Amy sat on the floor in the bedroom she shared with Julie at their grandparent's ranch. Julie sat nearby, felt the anger burning her face as she gazed at her sister, seeing her greenish blackened eye and Amy's cheekbone bruised to a deep purple. She remembered the scene as Derek apologized to Amy in front of both his grandparents and Julie. He promised to leave his sister alone, if she kept her nasty comments to herself.

ℰ⅁

Later, the grandparents asked Amy and Derek to go to their rooms so they could talk with Julie.

"I can feel the anger, in this room, where this fight happened," Grandma Thurston commented as she and her granddad sat with Julie in the large open ranch kitchen, "still feel it. I warned Amy and Derek both that if they didn't settle down, Child Protective Services would come in and take them away from the family, to separate foster care. This is an awful burden to place on you, Julie."

"What choice have I got?"

Her grandparents watched her flush a deep red.

"You have an obligation to help your dad out. We're supportive but we will not tolerate any violence. They'll have to learn to work it out."

"Maybe foster care would be best."

"We hope it won't resort to that," Granddad Thurston shook his head.

In spite of what happened to her siblings Julie had a pleasant stay with her grandparents. She got to ride her favorite horse, Fancy Free, and she helped drive tractor with an older cousin.

She and her granddad spent time together while they mended fence. Granddad talked with her about how his grandfather homesteaded the land that they walked on now, where he lived his life. The easy wind caught her hair as well as his shaggy locks. Julie noted that his hair remained the same blonde she always remembered. She paused in moving the fencepost closer to him. In the background she heard a meadowlark pronouncing its song.

"Granddad, your granddad, what a strong person he had to have been, to take raw prairie and make it his dream. I'm reading about another strong person; her name was Helen Keller."

"Yes, I know a little about her, Julie, tell me."

"Wow, she may have had handicaps, but she still said some really good stuff, like wanting to accomplish great tasks, but what she needed to do was accomplish humble tasks, like they were great. Being blind and not being able to hear didn't slow her down."

Her granddad laid down the barb wire and came to her. They hugged.

"Granddad, I'll do my humble tasks, move my little family along. Mom's gone; dad's at work always. I want to be like Helen; what an awesome woman she became."

Her granddad nodded to her and smiled, "Be like Helen."

"Outside, here, that does it for me," she would tell her grandma as they helped prepare dinner each evening. "And granddad, he lets me drive the pickup to get to and from mending fence."

"I'm glad, Julie, just keep doing your outside thing, back home, you know, walks," her grandma spoke in an encouraging voice as she patted her granddaughter's arm.

Rich Thurston picked up Julie and Amy after their time with his folks. Derek stayed on for another week, as requested by the grandparents. They helped him work on his anger issues. After that Derek came back to the family home in Empireville. He talked to his dad and sisters about his actions and made promises to them all. School started, and on September 20th Julie, now a junior, turned 16 and got her driver's license. Her dad bought a sturdy used car Julie drove to get back and forth to the high school she and Amy attended. Derek walked the couple of blocks to the middle school where he was a seventh grader.

Cheri called and talked to her children twice since she moved away. Before she left she already had a job at the hospital in the community where she now lived. Julie talked to her about the fighting.

"They'll have to suffer the consequences. I'm in no position to take either one of them right now. Foster care may be what'll have to happen," she said as she spoke to Julie near the end of the conversation.

The younger children had stepped away from the phone.

"You prepared me well for taking over, Mom. Dad cooks on Thursday night, or takes us out. I cook three nights, Derek Saturday, and Amy Tuesday and Friday. Fridays are still pizza nights. You know how we love pizza. We do simple stuff like we always have. Housekeeping chores, we got them divided up. Between Amy and me we keep the wash caught up. Each of us kids cleans a bathroom, since we got three of them. And we keep up our own rooms, me the kitchen and living room. Derek's doing the lawn mowing; he's big enough and he likes being outside, like when we were at Granddad's. Life skills, I'm definitely learning life skills, and so are they."

"I'm so glad, Julie. You're my girl, my follow-through kid, you're pretty amazing, keeping up with your school work and managing home."

"I'm still taking guitar and still sing. Oh, and your roses," she paused, bringing up the roses in her memory, "that you love so much, they're blooming again. I'll cut them just a little and show Amy how to mound them, like I saw you do, this fall. And, Jace, oh my gosh, is so great; we go to church together on Sundays. Sometimes Amy and Derek come along. Jace's already so excited about his mission when he graduates. He loves serving his church. Mom, he's so good for me."

"I saw that first hand, Julie."

℘

"How're your classes going?" her counselor, Mrs. Warren, asked as Halloween neared.

"Calculus, chemistry, physics, Spanish III, and a'course English and History, it's all good. Mrs. Warren, I gotta share what I'm planning to do."

She felt big tears spring into her eyes, burning them. Her throat ached as she tried to talk.

"Take your time, Julie."

She cleared her throat and began, "I've so much anger, my parents splitting up, we're with dad. Mom's down south, workin' at a small hospital outside of Vegas. She loves what she's doin', finished her training as a CNA a few months ago. Every time I talk to her I want to say terrible things. But I know it won't help. It'll just make her hate me. So I got a plan, sounds like I'm runnin' from everything. And yeah, in a sense I am, 'cause I can't take it anymore."

Mrs. Warren heard the sharp tone to her voice. Julie went on to explain how she planned to spend her spring semester and also about her siblings' fighting.

"Absolutely, Julie, that is all very possible for you to do. You are motivated; you're saying your dad he'll pay for your preps at the CC. And it's totally smart that you're prepping for the GED test, and at the same time prepping for taking your ACT and SAT. I think you will soon decide that college is where you're headed. A lot of students forget when they get their GED that the scores on the college boards are an important item colleges look at for admittance."

Julie watched her counselor smile; the first smile she'd seen since they began the difficult conversation.

"And you'll have all your scores, GED, ACT, SAT, good for you."

"Mrs. Warren, not just immediately, but after I get established, you're right, college may be for me. I just don't know what I'll study, or where, or exactly when. And my biggest worry is the cost of my future education. Dad's not gonna help out; I know that for sure. Right now I'm grateful that he's given me a car to drive and is paying for my insurance, eeeuuuwww, expensive."

One final question, Julie, does he know your plan?"

"Yes, he insists I'll change my mind. And he appreciates that I've helped out so much. Amy'll take over. Once I leave I know the only help I'll get is with my car."

"You haven't shared what you plan to do, where you're headed. Is it something your dad is OK with?"

"Yeah, oh Mrs. Warren I'm taking CPR and First Aid right now, that's so I can enroll with two or three Nanny Services, who like send nannies to Idaho and Montana. That bit of medical training will be important, since I'll be not quite 17 next summer."

"So what ages are you thinking of working with?"

"Not tiny babies, uh, little kids, like kindergarten to near middle school. They still listen, not like older ones."

"It's a fine goal, live with the family?"

"Only if I have to; I'll work long hours and days; I want a place of my own, at least to crash at night. I'm excited about it; know it's a first step on my journey."

"Keep me informed, Julie; come to me when you need to. I'm giving you my business card and home cell phone. You can count on me, please."

Mrs. Warren came from around her desk and she and Julie hugged.

As Julie stepped back from her, the counselor again saw tears in Julie's eyes.

"Do you have folks to talk to?"

Julie nodded her head, "Jace, the special boy in my life, our youth minister at our ward, I've just asked him to keep our family in his prayers 'cause we're goin' through a rough patch. And," she paused, her eyes widening to Andrea Warren, "my granddad, dad's dad, he's a great listener, a wise man, and of course, you."

Mrs. Warren saw a small smile appear on Julie's face as she thanked her for the talk.

&

"So now you know, Jace."

"Hey, baby, this is a special time, Christmas. I'm sorry for all the family issues you face. But," he put his hand under her chin, lifted her face and kissed her full on the lips, "you are super positive, know where you're headed, got goals."

"Will you help me with my DVD of introduction for prospective parents?"

"Course, I'm cool with video stuff; you just write the script. We'll rehearse it, then I'll record you for the DVD. We should make at least five or six copies."

"OK if we do that in January? Cause I'll be in CC prep classes most of the semester."

"You're definitely leaving high school after your final exams; you won't see me play any more basketball games, like tonight?"

They sat together in his car in front of the Thurston home. His eyes searched hers. He saw the emphatic shake of her head.

"I got studying, I mean it'll be every evening; I'm all set up with my classes at CC. Mrs. Warren and I sat down; she's helped me with everything. Dad's gonna pay for the classes, my big Christmas present."

Jace and Julie hugged at her front door.

"Happy Christmas, baby."

"I love you, Jace."

"And I love you."

&

Julie lay on her bed, listening to a holiday CD. Her dad would be home soon from his shift. She heard her brother and sister, their voices raised. Soon they screamed at each other.

"Don't step in, Julie, they have to learn to work it out," she told herself. She heard crashing and screams from both of them. She kept her door closed and locked. Then she heard her dad's voice. She also could hear the punches and the kicks. The screaming stopped. She heard her dad lower his voice and whimpers come from her brother and sister. Soon it was silent. Julie stepped out and grabbed the cell phone in the kitchen. She peeked around the corner into the living room. She saw the handsome Douglas fir lying on the carpet. Amy was next to the tree with Derek nearby. And her dad, she saw him sitting with his head in his hands.

"Oh dear God, I don't want to call Jace 'cause that'll stir up his whole family, and I don't have a girl as a friend that I'd want to burden her with this mess."

Then she thought of her counselor. Her voice trembled as she phoned Mrs. Warren, who happened to still be up. Julie told her what she first heard, and then saw. Within several minutes Julie heard the screams of sirens, not her siblings. The ambulances took them away. Her dad left in a police car. Julie gave her statement to the one policeman who stayed behind. He made sure the whole scene got photographed.

"This mess, OK?" she pointed a hand over the chaos.

"Good, go ahead and clean up," the investigating officer nodded to her.

Julie called Mrs. Warren back, as Mrs. Warren had asked her to do. She thanked her for calling 911.

"We're in God's hands, Mrs. Warren."

"Right, Julie, yes we are, now and forever." Mrs. Warren paused, "what now? I hear your voice, it's not as trembling as when you called earlier."

"Yeah, clearly I'm so angry, not going to bed yet, I'll clean up, think dad'll go to jail and Amy and Derek will go to separate foster care when they get out of the hospital."

"To prepare you, Julie, from the cases I've known, I suspect they'll eventually come back to your home; but there'll be counseling for everyone."

"That's so important, 'cause somebody's gonna die, otherwise."

Julie stood in front of the ruined Christmas tree. She felt her whole body shake from the sadness and anger within her. She ran to the bathroom to try and vomit, but nothing came up. After she put water on her face and started taking deep breaths through her nose, she started to feel better.

It took her some time to remove what was left of the Christmas ornaments from the trashed tree. Julie put the presents that were not smashed into the family member's room. She picked up the pieces of broken ornaments, sponged up the spilled water from the tree and applied a vinegar and baking soda mixture to remove bloodstains from the carpet.

"My sister's blood, from her face," she cried out, "Dear God, guide and protect this family."

Out in the garage she used a maul to chop the tree up and put it in the trash container. At 1:30 she turned on Christmas music, vacuumed the now nearly dried carpet, and made the living room presentable. Very little of Christmas remained, because the tree was the attraction.

"The consequences of actions, my family's gotta learn that," she told herself, "for me too," she sobbed as she headed for her room.

Julie slept at about 2:30. At 7 a.m. the hospital called to let her know they were keeping Amy and Derek one more day. Her dad showed up at 7:30, showered, got into his car and left. He did not talk to Julie. She left the home and drove to school, like always.

By the end of the day Julie felt like a zombie, not really in control of her mind or emotions. Jace followed her home in his car. He held her close while she told what she heard, and then saw, when she came from the kitchen the night before. Jace looked around the quiet living room, not comprehending what had happened there the night before.

"It's so ugly, Jace, happening at this most glorious time of year, Christ's coming into the world."

"Chin up, baby, you're a survivor, let this go, as best you can. He's in charge," Jace spoke as he looked upward.

"Right."

Jace helped her dig out a coffee maker that came out when the family had guests who drank coffee. Together they made coffee. They each drank a half cup of the hot stuff.

"The coffee, it warms me, makes me feel better, thanks Jace, just a couple more days, finals, Christmas coming."

They hugged, and he left. Tears flooded his face after he got into his car. He let the sadness he felt for Julie and her family take him for a minute. Deep sobs wrenched his throat.

"Dear God, continue to watch over Julie, and her whole family. I pray and pray, help them, God."

ℴℴ

After school the next day Julie picked Amy up from the hospital. Their dad had been in earlier to sign Amy's release papers. Julie observed the heavy patches bandaged over her eyes. Amy had corneal scratches on both her eyes, plus oozing wounds where Derek jammed her face, again and again, into the boughs of the Christmas tree. The next day, if the opthalmologist deemed it OK, the bandages would come off. Amy could return to school for finals. Derek left the hospital for a juvenile detention facility.

Her dad did not speak to her of the incident with her brother and sister. Julie decided that passing time might answer the question of what would happen to Rich Thurston.

"Granddad, you and grandma, you know the story?" Julie asked after she phoned her grandparents.

"Yes, child, your dad called us very early the next morning after it happened and told us. We decided to invite him and you girls to spend Christmas day with us, our usual gathering with some of our neighbors. It's a lighthearted time, lots of fun and a potluck. You and I will talk later; your dad told us he hadn't shared with you yet."

"Thank you, Granddad, for everything."

"God bless and keep you, child."

She felt restless after her phone call so Julie put on her coat, hat, gloves, boots and went for a walk. She saw a light dusting of snow from earlier in the evening. She gazed up to the night sky glistening with sparkling stars everywhere. She turned to find the Milky Way.

"God, thank you for keeping the sky the same, there's a consistency out here that helps keep me anchored. I just gotta keep doing my humble task, me and like Helen did, 'cause one day before long it'll get me to my great task, that's a job, and then making money to help with, yeah, I've decided, my college education. I felt real confident every time I cleaned Amy's wounds on her face and around her eyes. I'm so relieved she can see OK. And the doc says there won't be any scarring on her face. Maybe I should look at health careers; what'cha think?"

She felt a little spring in her step as she made her way back home. A few of her neighbors had outside Christmas lights turned on.

"That's so welcoming, the lights, thanks neighbors," she spoke out.

She unlocked the front door of their darkened house, deciding that she would begin keeping the front porch light on at night, for as long as she remained in the home. The Thurston family wanted to delay opening presents until they got back from the grandparents.

Julie and Amy helped their grandparents with the neighborhood potluck at noon on Christmas day. Amy told anyone who asked her about her face what happened. The replies she got were sympathetic. She told Julie how much it helped just to talk it out. The teens agreed that counseling would be essential for the whole family to heal.

Julie had fun; she knew several of the neighbors from the years she spent on her granddad's ranch outside of Twin Trails, Idaho. Everyone concentrated on this special day of celebration with lots of food and conversation. The three of them left early in the evening.

"I'm so glad we came," Amy agreed once they got in the car and headed down south and east to Empireville.

"I enjoyed it," their dad spoke up. "And ladies, you need to know what's going on in my life, and in your brother's."

He explained being let out of jail on his own recognizance. Rich never had so much as a speeding ticket his entire life. Plus his ward's minister came to the police station to counsel him. That man brought Rich home the morning after the incident. So Julie finally figured out how her dad got home. Their brother would be released from the juvenile facility to be placed in a foster care situation for an unspecified period, with anger management counseling. A whole team of professionals would work with Derek and the rest of the Thurston family.

Julie loved not having to go to high school. She had casual friendships with two girls, but nobody like Jace. She appreciated the adult-like attitude of her teachers at the community college. Her counselor there had some familiarity with the home situation Julie had. From the way her teachers talked about her rapid progress, she would be ready to take her GED exam in April and the ACT and SAT exams soon after that. Julie left home at 7:45 every morning, Monday through Friday. She studied in the library when she was not in class. She returned home every afternoon at 4:15. That gave her time to accomplish her chores in the home and practice her guitar. She even wrote the melody for a song she learned to play on the guitar. She surprised herself because she never thought she had that kind of ability. Eventually the lyrics came to her.

Jace kept his promise, helping her produce a DVD of introduction to parents who needed a nanny. In the DVD she sang one stanza of her new song while playing her guitar. Her prospective employers knew about her future plans, her reasons for getting the GED and having her ACT and SAT scores available, that college was on the horizon for her. She spoke in blunt terms about both her family and her financial situations, that there would be no assistance except for financial aid, when she decided on college. Julie needed a job where she could save money for her education. She explained her skills, her CPR and First Aid training, and the two letters of reference from the families with whom she babysat over the past few years.

In late April she concluded her work at the CC. Her GED scores as well as her ACT and SAT scores turned out to be excellent. At that time she applied to four different nanny agencies who worked with families in the Idaho and Montana areas. That's where she decided to be.

One agency turned her down flat because she would only be 17 in September. Two others said maybe to interviewing her, and one agency wanted to interview her by phone after they saw her DVD. Jace stood beside her, step for step as she made her way through the semester at CC.

Shortly after Julie started at the CC she would always say to Jace, "We gotta go about the business of living, God's with me."

It became the way they would end many of their phone conversations and times being together.

"Jace's the best thing in my life during this time. He's a student, great grades, plays football, basketball, and runs track. He'll be going to BYU after his mission. I know he'll get in there. He talks about that university to me since forever," her thoughts spun out as she drove home from the CC for the last time.

They spent their school years at the same schools, from kindergarten 'til now. Jace and Julie were best friends and fell in love when they were 14.

She already told him, "Start seeing other girls; you gotta go on with your life. I am, for reals, leaving."

Jace felt a burning ache in his heart as she made that statement to him. He saw the blaze of her brown eyes.

"She really is going away and I can't even open my mouth right now to let her know how I feel," he thought to himself as they hugged.

2

He held the DVD and put it back in its plastic cover.

"After watching this twice, once with Amy and then by myself, I already know who I want to watch over Katie and Annie. This young lady, Julie, will meet our needs nicely," he spoke out. "The other women we've interviewed don't hold a candle to her."

Jack Reinert went to their rooms and gave each of his daughters a goodnight hug and kiss. He joined his wife in the kitchen. They poured themselves white wine. He put Julie's DVD on the table.

"It's gonna be quite a transition. You spent a lot of time with the girls during your sabbatical this past nine months.

"Whoa Jack, not that much, remember my research work at the Southern Center. I was gone for several days at a time. But yeah, now I'll be packed with work. The department has me teaching three classes this fall and two in the spring. We need a six-day-a-week nanny. She's gotta have Sunday off; we'll be working her 72 hours a week, 7 to 7. If we decide on Julie, I want her to have like a studio apartment, a place nearby. She will need time away from us at night. I've got the girls lined up with activities after school four days a week. Friday, they'll get a break. But Saturday they both will always have dance and gymnastics, plus church class. Sunday's church and afternoon skiing in the winter. Julie mentioned in her DVD that Friday night was pizza night at her house. That sounds like a great way to finish off a week. Wha'cha think?"

"Agreed," they touched their glasses together and took one last sip of their wine.

&

From the information her nanny service provided, Julie thought this might be a situation she would like. Earlier she talked with Amy Reinert on the phone.

Amy asked her about her home management style.

"Both my letters of reference mentioned my helping the children in my care learn tasks around the home, cleaning up after meals, getting rooms in order for bed, that kind of thing, responsibilities appropriate to their ages."

"Yes, Julie we read that. You talked about life skills in your DVD, and you are certainly doing that with both youngsters you babysit and your brother and sister at home."

"Right, team approach is how I handle everything I do; everyone helps out so that they feel they've contributed. With your girls their homework is most important. I imagine Annie will have some, even in kindergarten. When we get home from their after-school activities, they will do homework. I cook simple meals, for the family. I'll provide a list once of week for what I need from the store to plan meals. You mentioned that Jack is your grocery shopper. Play comes after homework for the girls, if it isn't dinnertime by then. I like your idea of dinner with your husband and the girls on Tuesdays, Fridays, and Saturdays. On Mondays, Wednesdays, and Thursdays the girls and I'll eat a little earlier, so they have their baths and are in PJ's when you folks get home. I'll fix you plates you can heat up later. Oh my gosh, I talkin' like I already have the job, but you need to know."

Julie drove to Brakerman, Montana, to meet the family in early August. She found Katie and Annie to be polite and helpful. She inspected the home and found it to be warm, friendly, orderly and clean. The girls showed her their rooms and the bathroom they shared. When the parents asked them for private time with Julie, they went to their rooms, Katie to read, and Annie to work on her drawings.

It was Julie's turn to ask questions. She wanted to know about Jack and Amy. They sat together on the back patio with Julie sitting across from them at the circle table. Julie drank her pop, and they sipped lemonade.

"You're both at the University?"

Jack nodded to Julie. He touched his wife's hand and smiled into her eyes. He shifted his gaze to Julie and then back to his wife.

"She's the light of my life."

Then he fell silent.

Julie felt a flutter in her chest, "This is what love looks like," she thought as her eyes started to mist.

"I'm 13 years older than Amy. I thought for sure I'd stay a bachelor. And then this young one came on board as a new faculty member in Plant Science. I'm faculty in the department of Animal Science, been there for some time. We both teach and do research," he gave a laugh, "that means we write lots of papers. I also work with graduate students in the Animal Science program. You'll meet some of them."

"You both have your doctorates; you're both Dr. Reinert?"

"That's correct, hey, we're not that formal around home," Amy giggled and nodded to her husband, "we're just Amy and Jack."

"Sounds like it's been hard for you, Amy, having two little ones, teaching, doing research. How've you done it all?"

"My parents lived here until a few weeks ago. That's how we did it. We had a few nannies, but my folks really carried the load. They wanted out of our cold winters. They live in Arizona now. The girls are old enough to pretty much handle themselves, and in just a short time, Annie's in all day kindergarten and Katie's in second grade. So life's getting easier with the children. Our lives," she smiled to Jack, "are just as crazy as ever. We want you to join our family, Julie, to help us with our girls."

Julie heard the serious tone in Amy's voice as she looked at her. She saw Amy's smile.

"Fill me in on the details, please."

"7 to 7 Monday through Saturday; we want you to have Sundays off, for church and to relax. You'll drive the girls to school and pick them up. They can walk home, the school's not far, but we prefer you pick them up. We have cold winter days," Amy smiled to her.

Julie nodded.

"I understand that there's no overtime; this is a nanny situation. You haven't mentioned about laundry and keeping up your home. I can certainly learn how you do the laundry procedures. I've run my parents' home for a while now; I can take over the housekeeping here. The secret is keeping things in their proper places, avoid clutter. You folks certainly do that here. You run an organized household."

It hit Amy then, "I been doing the housekeeping, with help from the girls; they can help a lot. It'd sure be nice to hand some of that chore over." She went on, "We want to pay for a place for you to stay at night and to crash on Sundays. I found this studio nearby in July and signed a year's contract on it. You mentioned you want to start taking classes. You've gone ahead and gotten your application to State in, along with your scores. We'll pay your tuition for a class this semester. If it works out and you don't seem overloaded with everything, we'll pay for two classes per semester after that for as long as you remain with us. I've checked in with admissions; I believe it's possible they can admit you as a late comer for the fall term. Maybe you'll find a class to take, and that fits with our family's schedule."

"Oh my gosh!"

They watched Julie's eyes light up as she nodded to them.

"Amy didn't mention it, but you must have a salary; you're working 72 hours a week for us. And you'll have two weeks off in the summer, paid, of course, so we get you back." He looked to his wife, and they both nodded to Julie. "You've told us you want to put money away for your university education. And by the way," he paused, "I talked to your dad, Rich. I felt a big concern, as a parent, about your age. He says you've worked hard, and you know what you want. He hopes it goes well, you helping us."

"I wasn't sure you would check in with him."

"We sure did."

Jack stated the amount they would pay Julie per hour, at least for the first six months, with more pay if everything worked out for the family and Julie.

"Yes, I agree with that amount. This is a way I can begin to put money away, so that one day, I can attend full time, with a lot of financial aid help."

"What do you think, Julie?"

She looked from one parent to the other, smiled and nodded, "I want very much to join your family. I'll help you, but in so many ways, you'll be helping me."

"Julie, we work with young people, mostly a little older than you, but we see the bright promise you exhibit," Jack nodded to her as she watched him smile.

Julie shot them her wide smile, "Thank you for that perception; I really want an education."

The girls gave Julie a closer inspection of their rooms, showed her the two guest bedrooms across the hall from theirs and their parents' bedroom and bathroom at the end of the hall. They took her to the first floor to see their parents' nice-sized study. Julie noticed the floor to ceiling bookshelves on all four walls. The shelves were filled with books, journals, and three-ring binder projects. She and the girls moved through the small living room that flowed into a kitchen, breakfast nook, and formal dining room. Finally they took her down the steps to a cozy family room with a piano, fireplace and television. They showed her the laundry room.

"Mom's taught us how to do laundry; we're momma's helpers," Annie spoke up with a proud tone in her voice.

"Good for you girls."

"We'll help you too," Katie said, "'cause we're a team around here, dad says," she nodded to Julie.

"We practice the piano, take lessons, and play a little bit down here in the family room; we have shelves for our stuff. Don't really spend much time in here, 'cause there's not much time to watch television, lots of activities," Katie nodded.

They showed Julie a small bathroom and out into the two car garage with three walls of shelving, floor to ceiling, all orderly. Four bikes hung from a corner of the ceiling.

"We have a special cubbie for our skis and all our winter stuff. You'll come skiing with us, Julie?" Annie asked.

"Not sure."

She thought back to the three times she went as a beginner skier.

Annie smiled as she took Julie's hand to lead her back to the kitchen.

"We're mostly in the kitchen; I'll do my homework here, but Katie has a desk in her bedroom, so she does homework there. Dad says I'll get a desk for my room when I go into first grade."

Julie heard the confidence in Annie's voice as she smiled to her.

Jack observed the way his daughters talked to Julie and showed her around.

"They already sense she's the one," Jack laughed to himself, "the three of them seem real comfortable together."

Julie went out to dinner with the Reinert's that evening. They chowed down on delicious food at the little Mexican restaurant the family liked.

"Just curious," she paused, "none of my business, but your neighborhood looks to be about thirty years old, like my neighborhood in Empireville. But your home, it's so bright, open, and like new."

Katie began, "Oh Julie, you're right, we changed a lot of stuff two years ago. It is like a brand new home, the yard too; oh Daddy is our yard man."

"Yeah, little one, I for sure am the yard man; what's a guy to do when you live with three females?"

The little smirk on his face caused all the females to laugh.

"We're the second generation of professor-types who live in these homes near the university, matter of fact, our area is called professor row. But they're lots of little kids, younger faculty living here now. And yes, our home had a tired and outdated look. Actually we moved in with my folks for one summer while our contractor gutted some areas of our home. We like the change," she nodded to her husband, "plan to stay here."

"Forever," Katie and Annie chimed in, giggling.

℘

Julie looked around the small bedroom where she was to spend the night. She noted the painting of the butterflies and the gray tone of the walls. The girls brought her a clean towel and washcloth and told her where linens were kept.

"I'll say good night now. You both have been great; little hostesses, making me feel comfortable in your home, thank you."

Each of the girls came to her with a hug and wished her goodnight. Julie took the linens and hung them up in the bathroom next door to her. She sat on the double bed. Before long she moved, kneeling on the floor next to the bed.

"Dear God, I really want this to work out. These folks act like they really care, about their girls, and about me. Working with educators, they're folks who understand the stuff I need to get started, a place, a chance to see how I do in classes I'll take. They're paying for all that, plus a salary and oh my gosh a place to stay. Thank you God, for Jack and Amy and them giving me an opportunity for success; I am so blessed. I am grateful, for sure."

Julie opened the wood blind so she could gaze out of the bedroom window. She saw many stars that night.

ℛ

Her sister, Amy, gave her a look of surprise.

"Oh my gosh, one week."

"We got a lot to go over, little sis."

They began two hours after Julie arrived home from her interview. That gave Julie time to wash a load of clothes and make order in her bedroom.

Julie made coffee and drank a cup of the strong stuff.

She and her sister sat together, going over how Amy would run the house.

"When did you start drinking coffee? Our family never drank the stuff."

"Jace and I had a cup after the Christmas situation. The caffeine is a pick me up I need sometimes. Hey Amy, I'm no longer even saying that I'm Mormon. I'll find some other worship situation, maybe even swing over to the Catholic church. My family in Brakerman is Catholic.

"So you may even have alcohol sometimes."

"Hey, that's possible."

"You and Jace, you stayed true to each other, abstinence, right?"

"Exactly, he's strong in his faith, sex for him will be in marriage. We've only kissed and caressed. Amy, I asked him to date others. He's gonna be a senior, another year of school, and then his mission, so the next three years are pretty much secured in his life. I'll be starting college this fall, if they let me in as a late comer."

"Do you think that's possible?"

"Uh huh, I do."

"Wow, my sister, a college student, that's amazing, you've worked really hard Julie, to get where you are. I guess you won't miss graduating, senior stuff."

"Yeah, a few regrets, but no, I had prom last year with Jace, so graduating, not a big deal. I'm so way beyond all that." Julie stopped, looked Amy in the eye and touched her arm, "Hey, Derek's been home a week. How's it going between you two?"

Amy saw her sister's eyes widen as she asked the loaded question.

"He's polite, cooperative; I think it's for the better for him. Whew, think his foster home was kinda a frightening experience. He hasn't said a word about all that. But his grades certainly improved last semester while he was in foster care."

"Sheez, maybe it made him appreciative of what he has here."

"Yeah, right Julie, does his chores, not complaining, going out for football at school, already starting to work out on his own."

"Good, he's a fair-sized guy, football's a place to put his energies, work out that rage he's had."

"Right, we're in counseling, dad, him and me, it's helping, I think."

"Counseling's court ordered, right?"

"Yeah, we have to do it; part of Dad's sentence, and Derek's too. Derek beat me up pretty good at Christmas, but Dad really messed up Derek, with the concussion. Child Protective Services is checking in on us for a year, makin' sure there's no abuse going on, between dad and Derek."

"Lots of anger has to be let go of."

Amy hugged Julie, "That's for sure. And Derek and I have to continue to go to church on Sunday now that you're leaving; Dad's ordered us to do that. He can't go, but he wants to make sure we go."

"Yeah, that's good you're going. Dad didn't say a word to me when I told him I wouldn't be attending our family church, except one last time with Jace.

ฆ

Julie called her mom. Cheri wished her well in her nanny position. She told Julie that the divorce was finalized and that she was relieved about that. An RN at the hospital where she worked took an interest in her.

"Dating?"

"Uuuhhh, hey, just starting, I totally forgot what dating was like. Your dad and I only dated a little while after high school and then we married. You came right away."

"So you never really had a chance to pursue a career."

"Nope, being a mother was my career; you three were my life. But now, that you're older, I totally loved going to school. Julie, I'm kinda finding my way. Your dad and me, well, it really fell apart for us. My guy wants me to progress, maybe work toward my RN. He did, was a medic in the military, decided that was for him, so when he got out, used his education benefits to get his RN."

"Mom, it would be, wow, so awesome, for you to get more training. Uh, somethin' in health is what interests me right now."

"Don't say nuthin' to your dad, but I would like to take back Amy and Derek, now that your life is in Montana. It'll be a tough road for them, seeing their dad so little, being by themselves so much. I know they really feel abandonment, from me, dad, and now you leaving. Julie, you were the glue that held the family together."

"Honestly, Mom, I think dad would be relieved. He's got a lot going on, besides us kids."

"Only bad thing, pulling Amy away from her friends, and just a couple of years left of school. But Baker City's a nice little town; she and her brother would readjust. Hey, one more thing, you're moving to very cold country, before you leave get your dad to buy you a new battery, have the car tuned up, radiator flushed and new antifreeze, wind shield wipers in good shape, wiper fluid. You got jumper cables in the trunk?"

"I do, and I check the spare tire to make sure it's got enough air and give the tires a visual look often. All the stuff you taught us about car maintenance, thanks Mom for training us."

"Yeah, Julie, you gotta be in survival mode, driving little children to and from school and their activities, just like I used to do for you. For winter, better keep a shovel in the trunk, just in case you get stuck."

"After all this time, I finally have some appreciation for all that you did for us, Mom. Now I'll do the same for others."

℘

She and Jace attended church together the last Sunday before Julie left.

"This is how I want to say goodbye, Jace. I'm standing at my car in this church parking lot, our whole lives ahead of us, me driving to my new one, and you, soon enough. You'll be driving, flying or both to your mission somewhere in the world," she paused, "it'll come soon."

She stood, her light hair swirling behind her in the breeze. He saw sunlight reflecting in her darkened eyes, raw with the emotion they both felt.

"Whoever our life partners will someday be, you, Julie, will be my model for what I want in a woman," he spoke in a whisper, close to her ear.

"And you for me," she whispered back.

"I love you, baby."

"And I love you, Jace."

They kissed. They felt the softness of each other's lips.

"God bless and keep us, my love," Jace stepped back.

Julie nodded and waved to him as he walked backwards away from her. He turned and hurried to his car, his eyes streaming tears.

Her tears started as she drove home, and she felt a grinding ache, deep in her chest.

"You'll remain in my heart, always, Jace."

She looked down at her hands. They gripped the steering wheel so hard her knuckles turned white. Then she remembered. They had not hugged before they left each other.

ℴ⁗

"Thanks so much for helping me with this gathering, Julie."

They stood across from each other at the island in the Reinert kitchen.

"Hey, I love doin' this kind of stuff, Amy. Notice that your daughters are lending a hand too."

"Team effort," they spoke in unison, laughing together.

Katie and Annie spread out the plastic silverware where their mom indicated it should go next to the paper plates on the table set up in the formal dining room.

"Napkins, we gotta get the napkins and put them here."

They found the napkins and brought them to the food table.

"Dad's students are really good guys. They're nice to us," Annie spoke up.

Katie came back with, "Dad wouldn't have any other kind of students. These guys (yeah there's one woman) are going on for graduate degrees."

"Maybe someday be professors like dad and mom?"

"That could be, let's go see what we need to do next."

The girls returned to the kitchen and helped bring out plates of barbecued beef, mounds and mounds of chicken wings, salad, puffy dinner rolls, and cut up baked tiny potatoes with their skins on. Julie put plates of cookies at a smaller table nearby. Amy would set out the ice cream soon.

ℴ⁗

Every year Jack Reinert had a beginning-of-the-year party for graduate students in the Animal Science program. He supervised many of them during their stay at State U. He also gave a party at the end of spring semester. Tate Hollister came promptly at four p.m., the appointed time of the party. Two pretty little girls greeted him at the door.

"I'm Katie, and this is my sister, Annie. Our dad is Jack Reinert. Come on in, meet everybody and fix yourself food. They shook hands with Tate and let him wander in by himself.

Jack welcomed him and introduced him to the students already gathered together and chowing down. Tate tried to remember everyone's names; they were mostly new faces for him. He fixed himself a plate of food. A very pretty blonde gal asked him for his preference of a drink. She gave him several choices, and he decided on a beer.

"I'll open it and bring it to you, want it in a glass?"

"No thanks, bottle's fine," he paused, "hey, I'm Tate, and you're?"

"Julie."

Tate plopped down on the floor near two other grad students. He spoke briefly to them, proud of himself for remembering their names.

"Julie, she's hot, young, she looks about 14 with that sweet innocent-looking face. I wonder if she's Jack's older daughter?" he asked himself.

He filled his plate up a second time. Julie sat nearby, getting up to replenish coffee and drinks.

"Mind if I join you here?"

"Sure, pull up a stool."

He sat and spoke to her after a few bites, "You a member of the Reinert family?"

"I'm Katie and Annie's nanny. I'm with them 7 to 7 Monday through Saturday. I'm also a new student, got in to State as a late comer, so lucky, taking a psych class, just that this fall. The Reinert's are helping me with school; I got no money for school."

"How's it goin' so far?"

He watched her nod, a serious look on her face, "One day at a time, the family and I are still getting acquainted. Amy and Jack, wow, super busy people, I really know I'm needed, get along real good with the little girls."

"They greeted me at the door; they're dolls. Jack better watch out when they get to be in their teens."

Julie smiled to him, "Yeah, that's for sure."

"Don't mean to pry, but you look real young to be a college student."

"I get that a lot; I'll turn 17 in a few days and I have one of those faces, you know, young," she gave him her wide smile.

"Dude, how've you done all that at your age?" his voice and eyes both inquired.

"'Cuse me, I gotta refill drinks, be right back."

Tate looked around the sunlight-filled home, "Feels like a big family here. Maybe that's what Dr. Reinert wants to impart to us, that we're a family," he thought.

She returned, "Quick answer, my folks split; mom moved out of town; dad's got custody of us, he's got one day off a week."

Tate gave her a questioning look and shook his head.

"He's in gaming, a casino cage manager."

She saw the puzzled look on Tate's face, "Uh, a casino cage, you know like a bank in the casino; when a customer comes to the window to cash in the chips he's won, the customer gets money back."

"OK," Tate nodded.

"The casino's in Empireville, Nevada, our home. We're kinda in the northeastern corner, not too far from Twin Trails, Idaho. I got a younger brother and sister, well, I'm their mother, or was. Opted out of that whole scene by doing my spring semester junior year of high school at our community college, studying for and getting my GED, prepped and took my ACT and SAT. Here I am."

"Here you are," he smiled to Julie.

"What about you?"

"Ranch kid, North Dakota, went to school there, accepted into the graduate program in Animal Science here at State. I'm honing in on beef breeding, bovine and meat diseases, hopefully work in the cattle industry somehow. For this school year I'm a student assistant in a dorm on campus. I get my room and board, that's such a huge deal, and a small stipend. I just kinda help watch over the mostly freshmen who live in the dorm. I got absolutely zero money, except what I made this summer, piss poor," he heard what he just said and shook his head to Julie, "sorry about that." She watched his face flush red, "Uh, college debt, but you get the idea. What do ya think you'll study?"

"Somethin' in health."

"Maybe nursing?"

She turned to him and nodded, "Possibility, for sure."

"Good talkin' to you, Julie. It would be fun to do something with you, on a Sunday afternoon, whew, you have so little time off," she saw his sympathetic nod and look. "Could I have your personal number?"

"I'm in class or working here, plus lots of driving and activities after school with the girls. Hey, has anybody told you that you look like a young and much bigger version of Kevin Costner?"

He gave her a laugh, "Yeah, I get that, especially from a little bit older gals." He paused, "Julie, I know you have a very busy life. And my gosh, you'll be really prepared when you have kids of your own."

"Hey, that's for sure."

She watched him stand as he shot her a pleasant smile. She took his empty plate for disposal and pointed out, "Cookies and ice cream over there."

He nodded to her and helped himself to one kind of ice cream and a cookie. He downed all that, sitting back on the stool next to Julie. She handed him an orange napkin with her cell number written on it.

"Hey, thanks for your number, uh, may as well go back for seconds, this chow is so good, dorm chow is OK, gotta be happy with it."

Julie watched him pile three scoops of chocolate ice cream in his bowl. With his other hand he grabbed a chocolate chip cookie.

Dr. Reinert gave a short talk about the departmental expectations, his individual thoughts and those of the other professors who advised graduate students. He spoke for all the professors associated with the program.

As Tate said his goodbyes at the end of the party, he thought, "Oh my gosh, this is such valuable information for me, for all of us in the graduate program. I bet what he talked about isn't all written down somewhere; I'll make notes right away from what I remember; I'm glad he asked us all to be together."

℘

"Thank you, Julie, you're an excellent hostess," Jack smiled to her as he helped Amy and her clean up after the party.

"And you," he hugged Amy, "Oh light of my life, I know how much you enjoy the students and the camaraderie."

"I do," she paused, "I don't think grad students in plant science have anything like this during the semester."

"Sounds like you have a real tradition in this party, Jack."

"I do, Julie, one I take serious," he nodded to her. She heard the firm tone of his baritone voice.

"The girls and I, we're headed out to the butterfly garden before it gets any later and cooler. Amy, I just think the garden's such a fabulous idea, the girls learn about flowers, and about butterflies. They talk a lot about what they see, hear, and smell out there."

Amy nodded to Julie.

"She's an absolutely special young woman," Amy thought as she gazed at Julie.

Annie brought her packet of colored pencils and her drawing pad. Katie brought her writing tablet and pencils. For the past several weeks the girls spent time in the butterfly garden, Katie writing about what she saw and Annie drawing butterflies she glimpsed coming to and fro. Annie sat in the grass near the center of the garden. Julie looked up to the sky often; the sun faded into the faraway mountain. She sat, keeping silent, reading over her notes from psych class.

About 15 minutes later she whispered to Katie, "Wanna tell me about the flowers you just wrote about?"

Katie pointed to the left side and in a quiet voice, so as not to disturb the butterflies, "The black-eyed susans and the Mexican sunflowers, see the yellow of the susans, and the orangish yellow of the sunflowers. Golly the butterflies really like them. I got their descriptions," she pointed to her writing.

Julie moved closer to Annie.

"Wow, that's so pretty, which one are you drawing?"

"What I saw when we first got out here, a lupine blue. And I'm starting on a swallowtail I just saw." She pointed to the drawing, "See light yellow with black on the edges of its wings."

"Here Julie, I just wrote about the asters over in the middle of the garden, so many colors, purple, white, pink, and yellow."

Julie looked over Katie's descriptions.

"What about these guys on the right, the tall ones?"

"Those are zinnias, the butterflies especially like the red zinnias, and I'm gonna write in a minute about the cornflowers, they're the tallest," Katie nodded to Julie.

"What do you think about asking Annie to draw some of the flowers?"

Katie smiled to Julie, "I will, that's such a good idea, maybe we could make a little book."

"Wow, that would be nice," Julie added as she nodded to Katie.

The girls went about their work for a while longer. Julie returned to her notes and studied. Then she looked around and remembered.

"We hafta water the garden and also the pumpkin patch."

She unwound the garden hose and brought it to the garden area.

"Girls, please take your pads and pencils inside. I'll start watering the garden. Do you want to help with the pumpkin patch?"

"Me," Annie announced.

"I'll help," Katie added.

Julie screwed on the spray attachment and slowly watered the flowers in the butterfly garden.

"Julie, they're all gonna die pretty soon, right?" Annie asked as she stood next to her.

Julie patted Annie's head, "That's right, little one, but they'll be back next year. You know what that kind of flower is?"

"Uh huh, Mom said prenals."

"You remember well, they're perennials, we'll hope to see them next spring."

"If they stay alive, the snow and cold."

"Your dad will cut them back, real close to the ground."

"Pretty soon."

Julie moved the hose to the pumpkin patch.

"Before I start watering, ya wanta check out the pumpkins, see how they're doing?"

The girls put their hands in to lift up the scratchy vines and glimpse the pumpkins. They looked through the patch again. Then they counted.

"Five, we have five pumpkins. We'll have to cut them from the vines pretty soon, 'cause we might have our first freeze before long," Katie mentioned.

"We have to decide when. Then what do you do with your pumpkins?"

Katie and Annie talked together for a minute.

"You get one to take home, something from us girls."

"Thank you Katie and Annie. That's so special that you think of me. I'll let you decide which one I get. I have a tiny place, so the smallest one might be best."

"We'll think about that."

"And the other four?"

"Two we keep in a cool place, not carved, so we have a special Thanksgiving decoration; we use dried Indian corn, mom helps. And we carve the other two, one for inside and the other for outside, to greet the trick-or-treaters who come to our house."

Julie gathered the girls together, one on each side of her.

"You know what?"

"What Julie?"

Your butterfly garden, it's so lovely, it's a small miracle, your helping hands with the soil and seeds, awesome what you've grown, and the pumpkins, so sweet to watch them plump up.

"We like it outside, Julie."

"Uuummm, me too."

℘

"These leftovers, wowzee delicious," Jack commented as the five of them sat at the formal dining room table. He insisted that they have dinner at the table, whether he and Amy were there or not. It had always been their family tradition. Everyone enjoyed the reheated ribs and wings. Amy made a salad because the students finished up every bit of the salad and piles of potatoes she fixed. The girls and Julie had their ice cream after they finished up their main plates.

"Yikes, three chocoholics," Julie smiled as she nodded to the girls and then pointed to herself. She heard giggles from the parents.

"Yeah, we know Julie, been that way since we could have fun stuff to eat. We started out with chocolate milk; mom moved us to chocolate ice cream. We just get a little bit, 'cause it's near bedtime."

"Yeah, quiet time before bed, that's super important, even on weekends."

"Julie."

Julie moved her eyes to the speaker, Amy.

"Yes, Amy?"

"The girls mentioned how much fun they have after they do their piano practicing. You work with them on new songs, singing, and you bring your guitar sometimes."

"Right, we're learning some cute little songs I've written for the little ones, simple melodies that the girls can play."

They all helped clear the table, load the dishwasher and wash up the few pans. Julie packed her backpack to get ready to leave. Amy came to her with the girls and Jack standing nearby.

"I want you to have this; it's a bit beat up and needs several new strings. Feel free to fix it up, bring it back, and you and the girls will have a guitar to go along with the piano. That way, Julie, you can keep your guitar at your place, and not have to bring it back and forth."

"Wow, thanks Amy."

Amy handed her the dusty guitar. Julie examined it, feeling the nicks in the finish and checking the missing strings. She could tell from what she knew about the instrument that this was an old guitar, and expensive.

"It was my mom's; but I never cared much about playing it. You have really sparked a musical interest in Annie and Katie."

"Hey, they like music; piano is important for learning the basics. I'll fix this guy up, bring it back, and, ok if I keep it in the corner of one of the spare bedrooms?"

"Sounds good, Julie."

3

"Cute little pumpkin," he patted the pumpkin that sat on the counter between the tiny kitchen and the rest of Julie's studio.

"Annie and Katie have a neato pumpkin patch. They promised me one pumpkin from their five-pumpkin patch. I helped them cut the vines attached to the pumpkins. That was tough going," she smiled to Tate.

"But you managed."

"Yeah, after we cleaned them up at the hose they took them in to the house. But that was only part of our task. Their dad asked them, with my help, to clean up the patch. They were real troopers, yanking and pulling vines from the ground. We had several garbage bags full of the remains. The girls showed him their efforts. He was pleased."

"You know the parents' story?"

"Uh huh, love story, wow, the love they have for each other's pretty visible. He calls her the light of his life." She paused, "Hey, please, that's private info, they're just a neat couple."

"He's some older?"

"Yeah, by 13 years, shared with me that he thought he'd never marry."

Julie smiled to Tate, "Until she came to State as a brand new prof in Plant Science, that's what he said, in front of Amy and me."

"Wow, a side of him I never expected."

"Yeah, and he's a super cool dad; being older, he's got an appreciation for his daughters, like that a younger dad might not have. My dad, so young, he's just mid-thirties, he sure didn't look at us the way Jack does with his girls."

Tate noticed her pressed lips as she shook her head to him.

Amy grabbed the guitar she needed help with, and they left her apartment for the guitar shop. Tate drove his small Ford pickup. Before they went into the shop, he put in his request.

"I'd really like to hear you play, your guitar, you sing too?"

"I do."

She paused and smiled to him.

"I'll give you a little concert when we get back with the fixed up guitar. This guitar Amy gave me is way more of an instrument than the thing I play. I'm not sure she realized what she was giving away."

"Expensive?"

"Yeah, back in the day, way over and above the cost of an everyday guitar."

Within 10 minutes of being in the shop the knowledgeable sales guy had the new strings added and the guitar tuned.

"Try it," he handed the guitar back to Julie when he finished.

Julie took the guitar and stood by a stool near the counter where the guitar got fixed, in the back part of the shop.

"Mind if I sit down here and check it out?"

The sales guy nodded to her.

She started by checking her procedure for tuning a guitar. Every note sounded true to her ear. She strummed the C, F, and G chords and heard the rich sound of the old wood against the strings.

Julie stopped and murmured, "Wow, this is a fine old guitar."

"Play for us."

She nodded to the guy and Tate, "This's somethin' from the Vietnam conflict, but's been around way longer, Civil War."

Where have All the Flowers Gone was one of the first songs she learned after taking guitar lessons for a little while. She played and sang several verses and then stopped as she sensed other people watching her besides Tate and the sales guy.

She heard clapping from the suddenly gathered audience. Julie felt her face flame red and hopped off the stool. She smiled to the audience. Tate followed her to the cashier and she paid for the strings.

"The tune-up's free; little lady, you can really play that thing, and your melodic voice, quite low for such a young gal as yourself."

The cashier smiled and handed her two business cards, "This one's a group that plays at a couple of the college hangouts. And the other, well it's a coffee house where folks jam several nights a week. Don't know what nights; and it changes. I'd suggest you check those scenes out."

Julie smiled, nodding to the cashier.

"Let me carry that for you, oh my gosh Julie, you play very well."

She heard the complimentary tone of his voice, "Thanks, took lessons for a couple of years, and kept it up. Now I write a bit, uh the melodies of songs; I work with Jack and Amy's little girls. The three of us are gonna do a presentation for their parents. We have so much fun, the girls and me."

Tate patted her shoulder with his free hand as they walked to his pickup.

He handed the guitar back to her and opened the passenger door for her.

"All in?" he asked, before he closed the door.

She gave him a thumb up.

They drove to her apartment complex and sat in his pickup after he parked.

"I'll walk you up to your place."

He turned to her.

"None of my business, Julie, but do you get lonesome, like today when you're not surrounded with the family and all the things going on at their home?"

"Yeah, I'm surprised at myself, but with the holidays coming up, I, I didn't realize what that part would mean, away from my birth family. I just wanted out so bad, but to answer your question, I have times of loneliness. I had a guy, back home, we'd gone to school together for years, belonged to the same church." She nodded her head to Tate, "He for sure was my first love. I had a tough couple of days before I left; we said goodbye in our church's parking lot on a Sunday. I left for here two days later. I've not communicated with him, told him to see other girls."

"God's will, it lined up with what you wanted," he gave her a solemn look.

She watched his blue eyes turn almost grayish.

"Yeah, God answered my prayer, gave me a new family, but I got lots of adjusting still to do. And I still gotta work on my sadness and anger; keep forgiving my mom and my dad, instead of fighting myself in my mind."

She paused as he saw tears come to her eyes, "Forgive, they did the best they could with us, 19 when I was born," she shook her head as she wiped away her tears.

She took a deep breath, "I know this; God's right beside me, staying pretty silent most of the time. But I do feel His presence, all day, each day, and that's what makes it all worthwhile, feeling like I have His approval, doing the right thing, like you said His will."

"You'll be with the family for Thanksgiving," he paused, "'course it's a work day for you?"

"Right, and Friday and Saturday, also work days, Saturday we're going skiing; only done skiing a couple of times, should be an interesting experience. Gosh, the ski area is pretty close; that's so nice. If I start to like it, I can go on Sunday afternoon."

She stopped talking and shook her head, "That's if I've done church and my studying. You ski?"

"I do," he nodded to her, "learned as a kid and kept it up since."

"Gotta head in; this's been fun; I like spending time with you, Tate. We both got so much going on."

They stood together in front of her place. She smiled to him.

"Hug?" she asked as she set the guitar against the side of the apartment.

"Oh yeah," Tate responded, giving her a wide smile.

They held each other close.

&

Julie sat in the back of the bright and cozy room, at the church where the younger Girl Scouts met every other Thursday. Annie sat with her group of Daisies, and Katie and her group of Brownies worked on a project. Julie thought back on her years of Girl Scouts, a good-sized group that her ward of the Mormon church helped with, the place where the girls met.

Being back with the Scouts helped her realize just how important that training was. She remembered the 3 C's with which the leaders helped her and all the girls: courage, confidence, and character. Julie always remembered being a leader in her different age groups of scouts. She knew the self-reliance she developed was a key to her coping with her family when the troubles started. Scouts taught her that she could make a difference, could make the world a better place. She saw that in the examples in the Journey books Annie and Katie worked in. They were young, but Julie knew that's when the seeds of helping out people and the world sprouted in little girls' heads.

&

"Wanta come trick or treating with us?"

"Sure, if you'd like me to."

"We just go in our neighborhood, and we have to put the candy we get away, except for two pieces. Then mom gives us candy as a special treat; it usually lasts until after Thanksgiving."

"Your mom's real smart about that, Annie and Katie. A couple of years I had serious tummy troubles from too much candy." Julie lowered her voice and whispered to the girls, "I was a complete piggy," she paused and said more loudly, "piggy."

The girls watched her cross her eyes and hold onto her tummy. She laughed at herself and the girls joined in the laughing.

Jack ended up walking along with the girls; he missed so many of these Halloween nights with his work. He and Julie stood back and watched the girls, both dressed as princesses, walk up the steps to the various homes in the neighborhood. Amy stayed back and handed out candy at the Reinert front door.

℘

"I'm not sure what I've gotten myself into," Amy stood in the kitchen as she prepared to leave for work the next morning.

"Tell me."

"Lots of folks here are havin' a hard time; another department person and I went to work with a couple of people in the human nutrition department and our student government group here at State." She stopped and nodded her head, "I was huge into Student Council in high school. We did some service work, like Girl Scouts do. I'm babbling," she paused again. "We're having a canned food drive for our Community Food Bank. The University's never participated before, and we think it's about time."

Amy gave Julie the date, a week from Thursday, and the location of the drive on campus.

"I'll be able to stop by and see it after my psych class. What exactly are you all doing?"

"All the cans of donated food will be placed at the outer boundaries of the University's Student Center courtyard. I don't know exactly what to expect, since this is the first effort. Once all the cans are displayed they'll be weighed before the Community Food Bank takes them all away to their facility. The whole school district is participating plus businesses in town, government folks, and the hospital, all bringing cans and nonperishable foods."

"How great for families who need help, Amy, and there are so many," Julie smiled to her.

"Hey, I gotta leave, I hugged the girls earlier."

After her exam the following Thursday, Julie took time to go to the Student Center.

"Unbelievable," she spoke out as she walked toward the Student Center. She saw can after can after can lined up along the boundary of the courtyard area. Photographers from the local newspaper and TV stations stood among the crowds of volunteers and students watching the event and taking pictures. Julie saw Amy way on the other side of the huge area as a Community Food Bank truck pulled up. Amy watched the cans being weighed and loaded on the truck by student volunteers.

Julie turned and walked back through the campus to the Reinert home. She would need to pick up Katie and Annie soon.

As she approached their home, she whispered, "So much good, God, it's wonderful to see such an effort as the food drive. It'll be a better Thanksgiving for folks."

෨

"I just heard from Amy. So this is my Thanksgiving call to you, Julie. How's it going?

"I'm busy, Mom, six days a week, up at 6, at Reinert's by 7, girls and I eat breakfast together; parents are usually out the door. That's after the girls dress and slick up their rooms. I help them decide the night before what they want to wear. We each fix our own breakfast and do our own cleanup. They eat hot lunch at school. I drive them to school, which is not far; deliver them at 7:45. When I get back I do my chore of the day plus a load of wash. Their mom and I plan meals two weeks ahead, so I know what to get out from the freezer. Jack's the grocery shopper. He and Amy have that whole process uber-organized. Oh, the girls help with the wash on Friday afternoons and share cleaning their own bathroom, then's our kind of free time, no classes for them after school on Fridays. We do something fun after chores.

I have psych class at 9:30 to 11 on Tuesdays and Thursdays. I like my class, a super professor, young, popular. So I'm lucky 'cause they live close; I walk into the university and to my class and walk back to their home. I have the rest of my time, to finish the day chore, and study or run personal stuff, or get dinner prep ready. It's definitely my time; Jack and Amy don't pile more stuff on me. Everything runs like clockwork, kinda like you always had it at home. Well, Monday, Wednesday and Friday are easier, no class for me, but often I'll go to the University Library to study or do research, or whatever I need to do.

I've met one guy, a grad student who came to Dr. Reinert's party at the beginning of the year. I like him; he's 23 so there's that age difference. He's got a ton going on, student in Ag Sciences. Oh, and I pick up the girls after 3:30, when school is out. They've got an awesome before and after leave off and pick up situation at their school. All drivers are sight identified by the school personnel, and I had to register, along with Amy and Jack, to be a certified person to pick up Katie and Annie. Even in a smaller community like this one, you can't be too careful with the little kids. Still, there are a lot who walk to school and a few who are bussed from farther away, a couple of black and hispanic kids. Mom, this community is very caucasian, unbelievable, not like Empireville, where there's some minorities who work different kinds of jobs, like in the casinos.

After school is when it gets tricky. The girls have a different activity every Monday through Thursday, some stuff every other week. Their mom and dad want them to be busy, and they sure are. Saturdays are crazy; they have their Catholic religious training, dance, and gymnastics. Especially Annie, who's five, gets pretty tired. Mom, I'm happy, moving slowly toward my goal of attending State full time, my humble task. The workload's pretty much like it was when you went down south."

"Honey, I have news."

"Mom?"

"I'm pregnant; Sam and I were married last weekend in a small chapel connected with the United Methodist church we both attend."

"Baby's due?"

"End of May, Rich's turning over custody of Amy and Derek to me at that time and will start paying child support on the kids. Amy and Derek will be moving down to Baker City."

"Have they met their stepdad?"

"Briefly."

"How's Amy taking the fact that she'll be a senior in a strange high school and a built-in babysitter for you."

"Not a word."

Julie began to feel anger and sadness puff up her head and her heart. She heard the "pump pump" of the blood coursing through the veins in her head. She knew she had to get off the phone or explode. In as quiet and pleasant a voice as she could muster she wished her mom a Happy Thanksgiving and hung up.

Julie sat down on a stool at the kitchen island after she poured herself a cup of coffee. When she stopped shaking from her anger, she held her coffee cup as tight as she could. She said the *Lord's Prayer* in her head as she drank the hot coffee in small sips. She looked at the time and knew she had a little while before she needed to pick up the girls. On this Tuesday afternoon before Thanksgiving she put on her coat, hat, and gloves and went for a walk in this neighborhood she liked so much. As she looked up past the skeletal trees she saw the sun smiling to her. She blew out a deep breath.

"Dear God," she prayed as she spoke out in the quiet, "thank you for making sure I'm in the right place, right now, on this day. I'm lucky, blessed, and grateful I've prepared myself for the next four years. I only pray that Amy will look at me, do what she has to do according to our folks, go south, graduate, and go on to college. She's got me, as an example. She's smart, makes great grades, works hard, has a little job now and seems to be able to run the house, get her school work done, and still have some semblance of a family life, just her and Derek, except on Thursdays, when they get to see dad.

God, you may think me awful, but I just could not congratulate mom on her marriage, or on having a baby. She's certainly made her bed, will have to live with it. God, guide me, today and through all my days."

It was then, on her walk home that she broke down. The tears flowed down her cheeks as she stepped up her walking pace to get to her car to go get the girls.

"Oh Amy," she whispered, "mom said that you didn't say a word. I know you gotta be angry on the inside; she's taking advantage of you, again. I'll pray for you always, that you'll be able to cope through all this; mom's marriage, a stepdad, a different community, home and school. It'll only be for a year, oh God, bless and keep my Amy."

As she dried her tears and drove slow to the school, she felt a quiet, a peace fall upon her, like a veil over her entire body.

Out loud she spoke, "I'll let Amy call me. God how blessed, how grateful I am for my own life."

ℂ

"Time for our special show for you, Mom and Dad," Katie announced after they finished their early afternoon Thanksgiving dinner.

"And something to give you," Annie added.

Katie played the piano, then Annie played. Julie accompanied them with her guitar and helped them sing.

They began:

"Autumn," Katie announced and then they played and sang, "floating floating coming down, orange and golden, red and brown, falling falling leaves."

"Winter," Annie said and then the singing, "snowflakes fall, He sends them, Dear God, I pray, I love you."

"Spring," Julie spoke and then the singing, "let's sing a song of sunshine, be happy and have fun on this bright spring day."

"Summer," Katie said and the singing, "oh butterfly, I see your wings. Go fly to the garden."

Katie and Annie presented their butterfly storybook to their mom and dad. They stood in front of their folks and explained about the artwork by Annie, and the story by Katie. Then they stepped back.

"And finally, Mom and Dad, here's what we sing each day on our way to school. Julie, you'll help us 'cause you always sing along?"

Julie nodded and smiled to the girls. She joined her voice with the girls as they sang,

"At school I'll work and play. Please help me today. I'll count on you. Help me God, in everything that I do."

Julie, Katie, and Annie came together in a hug and bowed to Jack and Amy.

Jack felt his throat engorge and ache. He could not utter a word. Tears came to his eyes. Amy cried.

"Our tears, they're tears of happiness, you three, your musical ability, and the book, thank you."

Both parents directed their eyes and their smiles to the three presenters.

Amy and Jack stood and moved to them. They gathered together in a great big hug.

"How wonderful, how grand, I'm remembering, this is what being in a family feels like," the thought pounded into Julie's brain.

ð

"A bunch of us are getting together to celebrate getting our grades done. Jack can't come because he has oral comps for one of his grad students who's finishing up."

"Fix Jack a plate for the frig?"

"Please, just for him; he'll be super hungry after a session like that. He'll be home by seven so you can go home. Your final went OK?"

Amy and Julie stood together in the kitchen that end-of-semester December morning.

"I aced the class."

Amy hugged her and whispered, "That's grand, Julie."

Annie and Katie stood watching the two women together. Once they said goodbye to their mom they came to Julie.

"That's great, Julie, liking college?" Annie asked.

"Uh huh, hafta study."

"But you're really smart," Katie added, giving Julie her confident wise smile.

ð

Later Julie looked at the clock in the kitchen.

"Man, I have so much free time. I got my chores all done, and I don't have to pick the girls up for an hour. I need to sit down and think of a small present to give each of the girls and then go buy it. Christmas is Saturday and they just have one more day of school before the break. Their parents insisted that I do nothing for them as Christmas presents. They said to save every cent."

She heard the doorbell ring. As she glanced out the side window, she saw a vehicle she did not recognize. She looked through the security hole and gasped. Julie opened the door and just stared.

In front of her stood a tall blonde young man with broad shoulders and an even wider grin on his face. She looked him up and down.

"Julie, it's me," she remembered something of his voice, from her past. "You're so beautiful, Montana's been good to you."

"Dear Lord, Jace, is that you?"

"One and the same, baby."

"Oh come in from the cold."

They hugged after she closed the door.

He lifted her up and swung her around.

They were both laughing as he set her down.

"You've grown taller, Jace."

"Yeah, another growth spurt, plus put on almost 20 pounds."

"What, why, oh my gosh, what brings you to Brakerman, Montana?"

He shook his head and gave her one of his lazy, memorable grins, "You bring me here. Your family invited me to stay with them tonight, the one night I'll be in town."

"Did they know you were coming?"

"Yeah, of course, a surprise for you, planned by your sis, Amy, your dad and of course, the Reinert's. I've got dad's car; we switched so I could have a reliable car for the drive up here from Empireville."

"Let me take your coat; you want to put your stuff in the guest room?"

"Sure."

"Follow me; I gotta watch the time; I pick up Katie and Annie from school."

He followed her up the stairs to the guest bedroom.

"I put your towel in the bathroom next door. I'll see you downstairs; something to drink?"

"Water's fine; I'm dehydrated."

Julie fixed him a big glass of water with ice cubes.

He drank it all down, standing in the kitchen with Julie nearby.

"Wanta come with me to school?"

"Sure."

As they drove the short distance and got in the car line to pick up the girls, Julie asked.

"Your semester, Jace?"

"A tough one, calc, it killed me, never had to study much, but this math is hard for me, wow, and then football, and now basketball. I'm exhausted and needing a break. It seemed real restful just to drive up here. Beautiful country, oh my gosh, and the dusting of snow all across the land, really it seems like Christmas."

Julie turned to him and smiled.

"And to see you, that's best of all."

He leaned across and gave her a caressing kiss.

"We're next."

Julie drove up. Katie and Annie got in the back seat as the school official closed the door and waved to Julie. They buckled up as Julie introduced Jace to them.

"Wow, you came all this way to see Julie," Annie spoke up from the back seat.

Jace turned and smiled to the girls.

"I did; she and I are good friends, since we were about your age."

"That's a rrreeeaaalllyyy long time," Katie dragged it out.

Everyone laughed as they drove home.

The girls took their backpacks to their rooms and came down for their afternoon snacks.

"Thanks Julie; did you help her with our carrots, Jace?"

"I did not; she had this all prepared for when you arrived home."

"We have piano practice and homework," Annie mentioned. "I'll practice first so Katie can start on her homework. We had our piano lessons yesterday."

The girls finished their carrots, applesauce and milk and got to work.

Jace watched the girls move out to whatever they were assigned to, "Wow, what an organized outfit. Is it always this way?"

"Yeah," Julie drawled, "I got them pretty well trained in the months I've been here, but their grandparents handled things pretty much the same way in previous years. Uh, Amy's parents, did most of the work with the little girls.

But they left for warmer climes, and now that Annie's in kindergarten all day, life's gotten a lot simpler."

"What's this?"

Jace pointed to the four candles encircled by tiny evergreen branches at the formal dining room table.

"It's an Advent wreath. They light a new candle each week of the Advent time. It's a coming of Christ kinda representation in the form of candles."

"And I see a Christmas crèche on the low table in the family room."

"Yeah, but Baby Jesus is missing. He'll come along Christmas Eve. This year Annie gets to present him to the Blessed Virgin and Joseph. This family is Catholic and they have some traditions, like not turning the Christmas tree lights on until after midnight, actually Christmas Day. They didn't put the tree up until a few days ago, another tradition. And there's more. Wanta hear?"

"Sure, this is all new stuff to me."

"And for Christmas Amy bakes a cake, chocolate, with the girls' help. It's a birthday cake for Baby Jesus, and they put white frosting on it, a symbol of Christ's purity."

"Wow, you're pretty well tuned in to this family's Christmas."

"Yeah, well I'm attending a Catholic church, one that's close to campus for everyone, but there's lots of students who attend. I like everything this religion does; it's kinda strict, like our growing-up church."

"You have every right to worship God as you see fit, Julie."

She came to him for a hug.

"I gotta check on Katie, and Annie's almost finished with practice."

₧

Katie and Annie sat across from Julie and Jace at the formal dining room table.

"You made a plate for Dad?"

"Right, Katie, and I made extra hamburgers, two extra and lots of French fries."

"You eat a lot, Jace, but, uh, you're a big guy, much bigger than dad."

"Yeah kid, I need the food, burn a lot of energy. I played football, and I'm on the basketball team. So food's fuel for my body."

They all watched Jace down his third hamburger and a small mound of fries. Everyone helped with cleanup after they had a cookie and ice cream. Katie took a quick shower, and Annie had her bath. They sat with Jace between them as he read *A Christmas Carol*. Julie checked the girls' outfits for tomorrow, the last day of school before the break. Their dad would look over their homework after he got home.

Jack arrived at seven and met Jace.

"Were you surprised, Julie?"

"Oh my gosh, Jack, thank you, what a nice gesture." She smiled to Jace, "To let him stay with you folks tonight. It's a great Christmas gift to see my friend again."

She nodded to Jack and patted Jace on the shoulder as he stood next to her.

"I'm going to show him the town and my place."

"I'll be back by 10:30; I gotta get back on the road tomorrow, gonna be playing in a basketball tournament tomorrow night and the next day, a tune-up for the season after Christmas," he nodded to Jack and then turned to Julie.

"We'll say goodnight to the girls; I'll be back at 7 to get them off to their last day of school until the New Year."

℠

Julie showed him Brakerman's downtown with its sparkling Christmas lights. They drove into State, and she showed him a few buildings.

"Welcome to my home," Julie announced as she unlocked the door to her tiny apartment.

Jace looked around as she turned on the range light over the stove.

"Coffee?"

"Decaf and only a little, you know we don't drink coffee, but I'll make an exception, 'cause it's warming."

He looked around and asked, "Is it furnished?"

"Oh, yeah, I had so little stuff; Amy and Jack've also given me a few things. I'm hoping to live in a dorm, once I get the money together, financial aid, I'll qualify for work study."

"So you'll be a nanny?"

"Possible for another year, then spring semester, I'll be full time. I can take a bunch of credits once I don't have all the responsibilities of a nanny."

They pulled two stuffed chairs together so they could look at each other. They sat with their coffee cups in their hands, sipping the savory brew.

"This place is tiny, but putting your bed where you have, it looks like a couch by day."

Julie laughed, "That's just exactly what it is; actually I spend a lot of time studying on the floor. I spread my notes out all around me."

"What're you taking next semester?"

"Chemistry 'specially for the health care students and rhetoric, it'll be a busy semester."

"Rhetoric?" he raised his eyebrows in question.

"Here it's a combo speech and writing to inform, persuade, motivate."

"Where're you headed, Julie?"

He took her free hand in his.

"Pretty sure, oh my gosh, Jace, I'm so excited, if I get the grades to be in the program, it'll be a BSN."

"Uh, that's?"

"Sorry, Bachelor of Science in Nursing, then I'll take boards and if I pass I'll also be a registered nurse."

"Wow, you know what you want; I'm still so unsure. All I can think about is my service to God and to my church for the two years after I graduate."

Julie watched him stare ahead above her, to something on the wall.

"Jules,"

"Yeah, Jace?"

"I gotta confess; I came because I just had to confirm in my own mind, my own Christmas present for this year that you were OK, that your life was moving on as you had thought it would, His will for you."

"And?"

"I'm happy for me," he paused and smiled to her, "I see that you are happy; working on forgiving your folks?"

"I am, Jace, and will have to continue to work on that for a long time. I guess they've done the best they could."

"I gotta get back to the Reinert's. I'll sleep easier tonight, knowing we both are where we need to be, me a high school senior, and you, a college freshman with your goal, your dream," he paused and looked into her eyes, pools of brown, "becoming true."

She helped him with his coat.

"I need another hug, Julie. Don't know if you remember, but when we left each other at the church parking lot last August, we didn't hug. It saddened me. And I missed this last semester without hearing from you. Thank you for the time you've been in my life, baby."

They hugged. He stepped back and she watched his lips press together and his blue eyes wash out into a sad gray. He started to walk away then turned around to her as she stood in the doorway. She gave him her wide smile as he waved. She waved back.

&

Granddad Thurston sat next to her in the comfy stuffed chair. They got home from his taking her out to dinner at the Mexican restaurant.

"Full?"

"Yeah, full to the brim, absolutely, thanks Granddad, decaf coffee?

"Love some."

They sat, sipping the hot brew.

"How was the semester?"

"Busy, just one class, A in my psych class; the girls had stellar grades at their school, and Annie already reads above the second grade level, so she's way ahead."

"And the parents?"

"Amy and Jack, very busy semester for them, Granddad, they understand teenagers and young adults. It's wonderful to work for them. And so nice that they let you stay with them tonight. Last week Amy's parents were here, such a blast, they're pretty high energy folks, just don't like the cold and snow. But we all went skiing."

"Like skiing?"

"I do, if I'm gonna stay here a bit, it's what lots of folks do, with a ski area so close by. Did ya have your gathering on Christmas Day?"

She turned to him, smiling in memory.

"Oh yes, we missed seeing you, your dad, brother and sister."

"I liked that so much last year; it was important that we be with family, to be surrounded by love, after the horrible evil of a few days before."

"And Christmas here?"

"The Reinert's certainly have their traditions, midnight mass, a Yule log burning along pretty good most of Christmas Day. Ham dinner, chocolate birthday cake for dessert, to celebrate Baby Jesus, awesome stuff, I got a pay raise. They're impressed with my work, how well it's going with the girls."

"And Jace, I heard he came."

"Oh Granddad," she touched his hand and smiled into his eyes, "just like you, he came to make sure I'd moved on, that I was happy. He told me I was his model for how he'd conduct himself through the rest of high school and his mission, to keep moving on toward his goals, college and beyond."

Julie drew in a deep breath and blew it out. She looked up, above the tiny Christmas tree that sat on the bookcase, and nodded, "We'll always love each other."

Julie turned and watched her granddad nod his head, "Ah, that first love," he paused in thought, "one never forgets."

Julie saw a spark, a moment of gleaming in her granddad's eyes.

"Exactly," she nodded, thinking of how potent that love was between her granddad and grandma.

4

Holidays, 2010

In every relationship with a guy Julie looked for what her grandparents had.

Trust, respect, caring, wanting to be with that person over and above anyone else; that propelled her grandparents through decade after decade of their lives.

Tate became her closest friend at State. But he moved on with his graduate degree in Animal Science. Now they communicated by e-mail. A fellow nursing student showed an interest in Julie, beginning with their second semester, junior year of nursing school. It started with a group of nursing students prepping for their exams. By now they were all lockstep into their program with the same classes.

"I've had my first love; he's been one of the best things in my life, and I will always love Jace."

She spoke with complete honesty about Jace after she and Ben Dunnoldson had their second date.

"Can't explain what I feel for you, Ben, except to say that you're blazing hot sexually for me. You're so intense, we've stood by each other and seen patients die, babies be born, shared so much sadness, then happiness, yanking our moods up and down like being on a teeter totter."

"You're beautiful Julie, you flame so hot as I touch you, feel you in my arms, you burn up."

"Yeah metabolism, and the sexual high I get just being around you, Ben. Not sure it's a good thing, the intensity we've got for each other. I want to have sex with you, but I'm struggling, 'cause I don't love you. For me, I think love needs to be part of the equation."

A few weeks later she walked with Ben back to their apartments.

"I've started my second month on birth control pills," she turned to him and squeezed his hand. They held hands for a few more steps. Ben stopped her, they hugged, and he picked her up and swung her around.

"We've got so much life to live, so many challenges in our studies this last semester before clinicals."

"That's right, Ben."

After that evening of revelation, they developed a routine where they could be together two nights a week. Ben always went home after to study or get ready for what the next school day would bring. They felt a wild excitement, exploring each other's bodies, discovering the many moods they had, brought on by the events of the school day and what they experienced in their training.

&8O

"Are you pleased with your internship assignment?"

Julie and Mrs. Kennishall sat across from each other in the coordinator's office.

"Yes, I know I put in this weird and special request, but it seems you and your group thought it would work out. It'll hopefully lead me to a nursing situation," she paused, "maybe the town close to my grandparents' place."

"You're lucky, Julie, to find this assignment, and such good news, it's one of our own, your clinical supervisor, she's from our nursing class three years before you."

They went on to discuss the particulars of Julie's assignment. It was the same discussion she and Ben had several days before finals began.

"Mountain Home, Air Force Base, where the heck is that Julie, St. Mark's as a component assignment, and where is Mountain Falls?"

"We could check it out on the computer, but I like to feel where I'm going."

Julie spread out her map of the western US as they talked in a secluded area of the University library. They sat next to each other. A feeling of sadness tugged at Julie's heart as she swallowed hard.

"I'm always telling people that I have care for that I'm moving on. So, yes, my mind is made up," she nodded her head to Ben.

He saw the bright blaze of her brown eyes. She showed him the base location.

"See, Idaho, a 10-bed hospital on base."

Julie pointed to Mountain Falls, a town 10 miles away.

"St. Mark's is a 25-bed hospital there. I'll work both hospitals. I'm so excited because I'll get to be part of it all, the elderly, newborns, families, teenagers, everything that happens in a community of 16,000 plus nursing in a military base hospital situation. That base is the home of the 366th Fighter Squadron."

"Wow, I think you'll have quite a few more experiences than I'm gonna have in my one-hospital internship in Brevatone."

"But you want to end up doing Emergency Room nursing. I think it'll be a good fit for you, Ben, since that's a fair-sized community."

"Yeah, 35,000."

"You'll get moved around a bit at the hospital."

He smiled to her, "According to my internship coordinator, they'll make sure I see it all."

"Just like I will." She paused, "Ben?"

"Yeah?"

"I gotta study, study, study, make those grades, get ready to go. I start January 1. This needs to be goodbye."

He took her hand and set their clasped hands on top of the map.

"What I've had with you, our caring for each other, it's been, well like we been," he paused, struggling, "we been like a waterfall running wild and free," he leaned to her and kissed her cheek.

He watched her nod to him.

"Gotta tell you, Julie, remember just a few weeks ago, you and me, I rode along with you. We'd just finished a gerontology unit at the assisted living center, on the way back to our apartments, when we came upon it."

"Oh dear Lord, I'll," she paused, "I can't ever forget."

They flashed back to that terrible afternoon. They listened to the cries of the injured little children and heard their stories. The school bus filled with third through fifth grade students headed to school after watching a children's theater production at the university. Ben and Julie cobbled together this story from the little kids.

"We need to stop," the bus driver heard from one of the teachers on the bus.

He pulled over, deciding to put on the red flashers. A car load of young people ignored the flashers and flew around the bus. That vehicle hit head on with another car that also chose to ignore the red flashing lights. The force hurled both cars into the bus, causing the bus to flip on its side and slide along a snowy highway shoulder. Julie and Ben observed the wreckage looming ahead.

"I'm headed to the bus; call 911, please Ben."

"Got it, I'll join you."

Four hours later they left the hospital, catching a ride back to their car parked on the side of the highway back away from the accident site.

&

They came back, sitting together in the University library.

"For sure, I'd never come across anything like that, Ben."

He put his arm around her shoulder and kissed her cheek.

"Way you handled yourself, Julie, I been in stuff like that during my Iraq tour, little kids are saddest situation. I was so proud of you; you kept helping children, off the bus, at the hospital. You're a brave healer, for sure."

She watched him as he looked way ahead at something in the library.

She heard his voice, hollow sounding like he was far away from her, "We'll make great nurses; I've got a vision of our futures."

He turned back to her; they saw tears form in each other's eyes.

"God bless and keep you, Julie."

"And God bless and keep you, Ben."

He watched her as she walked away from him, there in the library where they spent so many hours together studying. She did not look back.

&

Julie peered out the window as she felt the plane lift, out and away from Reno. It was the second leg of her flight from Brakerman for this Christmas time. Her mind drifted back to the conversation she had with her granddad her first Christmas at State. He drove, from the family ranch outside Twin Trails. He came, to make sure she was OK, moving ahead to her next humble task of school.

Granddad Thurston always had a special niche in his heart for Julie, his first grandchild. Theirs had been an instant bond from the first time they saw each other. Julie was a toddler and talked early. That first time she recognized him from pictures. She stood outside in the sunshine and looked up and up and up to see a very tall man wearing a brown cowboy hat. She pointed her tiny finger up and spoke out emphatically, "My Gran."

Tears came to Julie's eyes as her mind rested on thoughts of him. He died, out riding his favorite horse on the land he worked so hard on and had fought so hard to keep in the family, the land he loved. That was a year ago.

She heard a young girl's laugh coming from seats toward the back of the plane.

"Reminds me of Annie and Katie," she whispered.

Amy and Jack asked her to help out in early December. She finished her next to last semester of nursing school. The Reinert's nanny had go home for a family emergency.

"Thank you for the music. Thank you for the songs I'm singing," Julie sang along with Annie and Katie as she drove them home from school.

She stayed for a week, long enough for Amy and Jack to attend a conference. Their nanny would be returning also.

"That was the perfect end to my semester," she thought as she moved down the concourse to the main terminal. "It was really my last one on campus, to spend that little bit of time with my sweet girls, Katie and Annie."

She saw Amy waving to her from an area nearly full of folks waiting for incoming Las Vegas passengers. They moved toward each other and hugged.

"You look," Amy paused, "wonderful."

"You too, little sis, how'd your semester go at Nevada-Reno?"

"Great, and yours?"

"I'm so ready to get into my hospital, actually hospitals, to start into the nitty gritty of taking care of sick folks."

Amy and Julie had not seen each other since Granddad Thurston's funeral. Julie felt a little surprise to see how much they now resembled each other, tall, long-haired, brown-eyed blonde young ladies, with the same welcoming smile.

"Dad?"

"Sheez, Julie, I guess you wouldn't know since you two talk so infrequently," Amy shook her head to her sister. She paused for a moment, "Oh, positive news, he's engaged, a lady new in Empireville a couple years ago, Dad's gone back to church 'cause she goes to our ward, has a kid in college, she's a little bit older than dad. I see your funny look, yeah dad has Sundays off now. I like her; she's funny and really good for dad. He's been sad for a long time, mom walking out, wanting out, us kids all leaving, hey at first he liked it, then the loneliness set in. The shock of granddad dying really threw him for months after."

"You said we had stuff to discuss, about Granddad Thurston."

"Yeah, that's before you leave and after mom's holiday celebration. Everyone'll pitch in, it'll be fun. Mom's changed; she's happier too. Sam, well he's one special guy, and Lily, she's a smart and sweet little girl."

"Unbelievable, we have a half-sister."

"Right, Sam, no kids, wasn't sure he'd ever even marry. Now he's got a hefty-sized step family and his own kid."

"This the car dad gave you?"

"Yeah, sturdy, reliable, just like the wheels he gave you."

"I'm so lost, Amy," Julie said as she shook her head at the endless rows of homes they drove through.

"No worries, we're not far off a main highway; it's an easy home to drive to."

"Amy, before we go in, want to thank you for the way you stepped up, without complaint; moving to Baker City, doing what both dad and mom wanted you to do, helping out, the baby and all, finishing high school with your amazing grades, and then on to the University three months later."

"It was you, Julie."

"Whatcha mean?"

They looked into each other eyes.

"You showed me, no matter what, we gotta move forward, God's with us, always, does no earthly good to complain. You're my shining example. And look at you now, almost a nurse, your clinical internship left, all those courses, you dug in, whew," she paused nodding to Julie, "accomplished so much."

&

Julie felt in a mellow mood that third and last day of her visit with her mom and family members who were new to her, Sam and Lily. She decided that a little child helped bring the spirit of Christmas to a family. Lily did that for everyone that year, with her aliveness, abundance of energy, her auburn hair flying and shining hazel eyes.

Amy, Derek and Julie joined their mom and Sam around the kitchen table for a last time to talk before they took Lily to child care and headed to the hospital for their shift.

"Your dad and I chatted, and I've filled Sam in. It's Grandma Thurston. She's decided to leave the ranch. It's too much for her, the flood of memories. Their hired man will take over for the time being. He's tuned in to all the finances, been runnin' the place for the last two years with just a little counseling from granddad."

"Where's Grandma going?"

"To a home she bought in Twin Trails with some of Granddad's insurance monies; it'll be an enormous change for her, but one she wants to make. From what your dad indicated, she's had a large estate auction to remove every nonessential thing from the ranch properties. Before granddad died they renovated most of their ranch home where they spent those many years. Your dad says it doesn't even look like the same place. Kids, she's getting ready to sell, on one condition."

"Tell us," Derek said.

"If nobody in the family wants to take it over, that's the condition."

"Dad?"

"He's absolutely not interested; neither is his brother, your uncle, or his two kids."

"So what you're saying, Mom, is that it's up to us, do any of us want to take over?" Amy looked from her brother to her sister.

"Not me, I'm still in school, and I hate little towns, like Twin Trails," Derek shook his head.

"I'm headed to a big city life," Amy added.

Everyone turned to Julie.

She wrestled with her granddad's suggestion that she step up, be a leader in the next generation of the Thurston family. Granddad Thurston talked about this during Julie's second year of nursing school at State.

"Hey might be interested in doing this, Julie, living on the ranch, it's close to town, working as a nurse in Twin Trails. Nursing, that's your dream, what you want. I've downsized running the ranch, especially the cattle. The place," he paused and thought, "yeah, it's all paid for, money set aside for the property taxes and upkeep. In the summer and fall there'd still be the folks coming for our trout fishing, hunting mule deer, antelope, and elk. And, we also have the game birds that the hunters come for."

She closed that memory of her granddad's talk, and Julie moved her eyes from one family member to the next.

"One more thing, Julie, your dad indicates that Grandma Thurston has complete confidence in you," Cheri added. "She's always felt, and continued to tell your dad and your granddad, that you, Julie, are the only person in this whole family who seems to be able to look, beyond, way beyond, what's going on right here and now. That's the way she feels about you."

Cheri nodded to her daughter, smiling to Julie.

"The most important semester of my life is coming up. I can't make a decision until I've finished and taken my boards for my RN. Grandma'll understand; I'll contact her."

"Of course, Julie, now Grandma'll be able to see at least a little into her future. I'll let your dad know what you've told us about your last semester."

"We have to head out," Sam spoke up.

Everyone hugged Lily, Cheri, and Sam.

"To the airport in an hour to drop you off, Julie?"

Yeah, that'll work fine, Amy."

ℂ

"How can I ever thank you for letting me stay with you and Uncle Harve in Mountain Falls?"

"You're family, Julie. I know your mom is super proud of you, doing all this completely on your own, making your own way. And we sure enjoyed your company, with our young'uns all grown and gone."

Julie watched her aunt smile, nodding to her. They hugged.

"One last cup of coffee before you head out?"

"Sure, Aunt Ellie, I haven't really shared much about my internship."

"You were here only a few hours each night; I worried a bit about you, but I kept telling myself, she's a nurse, she'll know when to sleep."

"Yeah, I really didn't take very good care of myself, until after that awful cold."

Her aunt noticed her shake her head.

"When did that happen, see I didn't even know?"

"Six weeks into the internship; middle of February, I felt like I knew my way around both the base hospital and St. Mark's in town. There was always snow, wherever I was, sure was glad I only had to go ten miles to the base from town. The road crews kept the highway plowed real good. I'd finished an orthopedic round at both locations. It was such a pleasure to work with young military men, who healed up so fast from the accidents they had, way different from the broken hips of the old folks back in Mountain Falls. Anyway, guess my resistance was down, caught just a terrific cold. A 'course I got on antibiotics 'cause it turned into a sinus infection real quick."

"Subject change, well, Julie, you turned a few heads on base. Lemesee, I recall at least three different pilots who came to the house to pick you up for a date."

"Had fun, nothin' serious, but want you to know that those pilots were very interested in a wife who would be a nurse. Each young man explained to me how easy it was for pilots with nurse wives. The wives almost always got placed in jobs as the pilots went from base to base."

"What ended your relationship with them, if I can ask, actually, it's none of my business?"

Julie nodded as she took a final sip of her coffee, "That's certainly OK. All of us, pilots and me, had to move on; I shared that I'd remain in the area and kinda what was happening, my new home. Have I shared with you, after graduation?"

"Naw, not really, it seemed your plans were up in the air, not settled."

Julie gave her aunt her wide smile, and Ellie saw the sparkle in her brown eyes.

"Back to State to graduate, RN boards're out of the way."

"And?"

"Talked to mom and dad, in the last two days, I accepted a nursing position at the regional medical center in Twin Trails."

Julie watched her aunt wrinkle her forehead.

"Good luck in your new position, but you've been in and out a lot, young lady."

"Right, so dad's mom, Grandma Thurston, here's what's happened, oh did you ever meet her?"

"Yes, several times, at family gatherings when Cheri invited us," Ellie paused, thinking back and nodding, "yes, a very gracious and beautiful lady."

"She still is. And she's sold her place, the Thurston ranch."

"Didn't your family homestead it," she paused, "it's sold?

Julie heard the questioning in her voice.

"Yeah, my ancestors homesteaded it. I'm taking it over, the only family member who wants it. Grandma's deeded me the ranch house, barn, a couple of outbuildings and several hundred acres, where the fly fishing streams are. So we'll still have the fly fishing operation. That's all that'll be left of the original homestead."

"Everybody else in the family, again none of my business, Julie?"

"Sure, my other family members involved now have their money from the sale of the rest of the ranch."

"So that takes care of it?"

"Yeah, only a little bit of Thurston land left. But I'm happy to report that a neighbor rancher is the buyer of the rest of the ranch. He's always wanted the Thurston place.

Now he can add it to his large spread, run the cattle he wants and take over the hunting operation granddad had. The family name got pretty well known over the many years for our quail, elk, and antelope hunting,"

Julie paused, reflecting on what she just told her aunt.

"Think everybody's happy over the way things have turned out, so far."

She smiled to her aunt, and her aunt nodded back to her.

"But especially, Aunt Ellie, grandma is super pleased that it's me taking over. I'm the family member my grandparents wanted for the ranch."

ॐ

Jack, Amy, Katie and Annie Reinert attended Julie's graduation from State. They met back at the Reinert's for cake and a champagne toast. Julie went on to another nursing graduate's party which most of the graduating class attended. Julie heard stories of all the places the nurses would go. She felt a warm glow move through her body, a happiness that had been missing from her life. She knew now that the choice she made felt like the correct one for her.

"I have a job, I have a job," she kept telling herself.

She spent the night with the Reinert family. The next morning Katie and Annie gave a little concert to honor Julie.

"Come here, it was fabulous, you two, your playing and singing are just awesome."

Julie held them close, "You're growing into such beautiful young ladies."

Annie stepped back, "Julie, I'm gonna be a nurse, just like you."

"That's wonderful," Julie clapped for Annie, "and you, Katie?"

"I want to sing, to dance," Katie smiled to Julie and moved her arms and legs in a graceful leap. Julie gave her exuberant applause.

The family fixed brunch together; Julie watched and helped set the table.

"Moved, Julie?"

"Uh huh, got everything in my car, gave away the few other things I had. Grandma Thurston left just a couple items in the home where I'll live."

"That's the renovated ranch home?" Jack asked.

"Right, on the main highway, just a mile out of Twin Trails."

After they chowed down, the family walked Julie out to her car for her trip from Montana down to Idaho.

All the family gave Julie hugs.

"Katie and I want to come and visit you, Julie."

Julie knelt down to Katie and Annie's height.

"And of course, you shall; your mom and dad've already mentioned that to me. It's not that far from Brakerman to Twin Trails."

Julie kissed each girl on the cheek.

"We love you, Julie," Katie said and she put her arm around her sister's shoulder.

"And I love you," she patted her hand over her heart as she smiled to the girls.

"Safe travels, we're so proud of you, Julie," Jack spoke up.

She nodded and fought back the tears until she was out of sight of the home.

"It's over, a mighty and very important part of my life. On to my next humble task, as Helen would say," Julie smiled through her tears as she found the highway to Twin Trails.

5

Four Months Later-October 2011

"Happy, Grandma?"

Natalie Thurston shifted her gaze from the land outside the great room window to Julie.

She nodded to her granddaughter, "Sure am. Question is, are you happy?"

"Very, Grandma, my happiness just keeps growing and growing," she smiled and squeezed her grandma's hand.

"You're the one, our grandchild who sees into the future, who seems to understand what Granddad and I wanted for all of you. Think the other family members are OK with their money, the division of monies from the sale of property?"

"Yeah, assume so, you haven't heard otherwise?"

"No complaints, just hope they sock some of it away, so yes, Julie, I am happy with the way everything's turned out."

Julie looked into her grandma's eyes, the same brown as her own.

"I love this home. With this all paid for, I can concentrate on paying off my student loans."

"Still looks mighty bare, Julie, you're gonna add furniture?"

"Yeah, one piece at a time, when I've the opportunity to think about all that. You really left everything in pristine condition, Grandma, no messes for me to clean up. And I really appreciate that you got new HVAC several years ago. With winter cold and hot summers, it'll really be appreciated. I turned on the furnace just twice since I moved in last June. It's toasty warm. And I've hardly used the air conditioning."

"That's a ranch, the heat stays on one level."

"What do you think about the new stain on the hardwood floors?"

"Smart choice, Julie, the darker color I had was impossible, showed every speck of dust. This lighter brown, more muted color, it's very nice."

Natalie gazed around the combined kitchen and great room space. "Where'd you stay while the workers redid the floors?"

"In the cottage as you come into the ranch, there're bathrooms, a partial kitchen, and several rooms to sleep in."

"Thanks for this delicious lunch, Julie. You're a fine cook, and it was fun that you picked me up to go to church with you. I'd like to do this again. You know I never really embraced the Mormon religion; it was granddad's situation. And I loved him. I went along with everything he wanted. But now, I really like the priest at the church you attend."

Julie nodded to her grandma.

"I'll take you home now; I got a lot to do before work tomorrow. I sure love having Sunday off."

"And your other day?"

"Tuesday, gosh, for the first two months I had a 3 to 11 shift with Monday and Wednesday off. Working 7 to 3, awesome; that's mostly when stuff happens."

Her grandma smiled to her, "You certainly like the action."

"Yeah, that's for sure."

ℰℓ

"It's your left foot; the horse kicked you good, two small breaks, from what I see by the X-rays. You looked at them too. You're not swelling up too bad; lucky for you."

"Sure hurts like heck, tiny bones, can't believe they can cause that much pain."

"Julie, show him the boot."

Aaron whiffed the strong antiseptic the doctor spread around on his foot, top, sides, and bottom. He patted it dry. He held on to the boot before she handed it to Aaron.

"First the sock, the sock will comfort you. In a day or two you'll not want to take it off, feels so good," Julie shot him a smile. "I'll send a spare pair of soft socks with you.

"And you are?"

He couldn't quite see her employee ID.

"Julie."

As much as his foot ached he gave Julie a long look, admiring her pretty face.

"Hey, thanks Julie, and Doc, for your help so far."

Julie helped him strap on the gray plastic boot, over his pant leg.

"Velcro straps?"

"Yeah, they hold really good."

"Your truck?"

"Automatic transmission, so this'll work great. I do all the work with my right foot."

"Let's stand you up and see how it feels."

With Julie on one side and the orthopedic doc on the other, they got Aaron to his feet from the side of the bed in the ER.

"See how it feels as you take a step."

He wobbled as he put his weight first on one foot and then on the broken one.

He stopped and let out a big breath, "Holy malolly, hurts like fury."

"OK, you'll need to use crutches, for a couple days, then a cane, probably six weeks for the boot and the cane. You have to keep ice on the foot to keep the swelling down, but you know that. Hey Doc, who's gonna handle your big animal cases?" Dr. Carey asked.

"I'll call on my big animal emergency contact, over in Chocta County, if I need help. Uh, he owes me."

Julie saw the emphatic nod of his head. As soon as he signed the release papers and hobbled with crutches making jerky steps to the emergency room exit, she pulled the fitted sheet and half sheet from the bed he just used. She removed the pillowcase and proceeded to clean the whole bed area with antiseptic wipes. She got the area ready for the next ER patient, then went to the computer next to the bed and input the data she needed to finish off Aaron's chart. She remembered that Dr. Carey called him doc. She looked at the patient's name again; it indicated Dr.

"OK," she thought, "he's gotta be a veterinarian. Guess that's maybe why he seemed so calm in here; still he's used to being the doc, not the patient."

Julie looked around and got ready for the next arrival. His face stayed in her memory, short dark reddish auburn hair, vibrant brown eyes, even when he was in pain, and a beautiful smile.

"That's one uber good looking dude," she nodded to herself.

⅋

Late in an afternoon that week the realtor who called some days ago met her at her ranch home. He brought along his client. Julie met them at her front door. She had coffee and cookies ready. What she heard the realtor say when he first called her was, "I have an interesting scenario for you, Julie."

She let them in and shook hands with Joe McDougal, the realtor. The man with Joe took off his brown cowboy hat and held it with his right hand. His left hand rested on a crutch. Julie looked down to see an orthopedic boot on his left foot and lower leg.

"It's you," he said as he took her all in.

A wonder struck him, "I want to kiss you good morning, for the rest of our lives."

The thought, it zapped a red-hot shock to his body. He shifted his position with his booted leg.

She heard the surprised tone of his voice. She lifted her head to him.

"He's taller, somehow, guess he's standing up straight now," Julie thought. She was unable to pull his name into her memory.

"Julie, this is Aaron Engleman."

Julie gave Aaron her wide and welcoming smile.

"Hi Aaron," she nodded to him, "how's the foot?"

"Son of a gun hurts, gotta go slow on puttin' weight on it."

"Just like Dr. Carey said."

"Right, I'm a terrible patient, too used to being the doc; havin' a heck of a time developing patience."

"Time," she nodded.

"Yeah, right," she saw him raise his eyebrows, "that's fer sure."

The three of them settled in with decaf coffee and oatmeal cookies.

Aaron told his story of his injured foot and how he and Julie met in the Emergency Room. Joe explained the realty scenario to Julie. Aaron added his comments. He spread out a crude drawing he made of what he thought might work out for his clinic. After they finished talking and having cookies, Julie asked that they walk out to the property in question so Joe and Aaron could further explain what Aaron envisioned.

"You remember Doc Finnigan?"

Aaron turned to Julie as he asked.

Julie nodded her head, as he watched her wide smile.

"Course, Granddad Thurston had him out to the ranch over the years, for our injured. And Grandma took the dogs to town for doctoring. You're replacing Doc?"

"Yeah, that's right, he's retired, and I'm needing a different scenario for the clinic, too crowded in the town center. Joe showed me your place a while ago, guess it was in the middle of your moving in. I have my eye on this cottage."

They walked to the location, just a few hundred feet into the ranch.

"It'll be perfect; I'd like to lease this cottage, make improvements if you would allow me, a sign at the turnoff to your home, and a sign as people get closer. If I could, I'd rent a bit of land around the cottage. Can we take a look inside?"

"'Course," Julie unlocked the door and let them enter first. She stayed back as Aaron and Joe made their way slowly through the empty cottage. Aaron kept referring to his crude drawing and making notes on the paper.

They came from the back to the front of the cottage.

"Possible to add on?" he directed his question to Julie.

"Get with a contractor, draw up your plans and your budget situation and let me know with your paperwork. I'll check with our family's lawyer, CPA, and insurance agent about what something like this would entail, you know, me leasing the building and land."

Both men nodded to her.

"Plans for the small barn that's between the cottage and set away from your home?"

"Not at this time, Aaron, it's empty. Grandma had the big barn deconstructed. It would'a been a mess to fix up, cost too much so she donated all the wood. Her estate sale helped sell the rest of the barn equipment."

Joe smiled to her, "Uh huh, I heard about that, amazing what can be recycled instead of dumped into a landfill."

"Uh," Aaron eyed Julie, "might it be possible to rent out a stall or two in this barn?"

Julie shook her head, "I don't know about that, hey, it's gettin' near dusk, so a quick look, OK? The lighting's not great on the inside of that area."

Aaron walked to all four corners inside the small barn. He and Joe conferred as they left the building. Julie heard the hum of their voices. She stood and watched as Aaron moved at a slow pace from the barn to the cottage.

He waved to her and spoke out, "Thanks, Julie, please do your checking and we'll get back to you on the cottage. There's so much possibility here."

She watched his smile, a new look of confidence on his face she had not seen before. Julie walked back to the front porch of her home. She paused before she went in.

She spoke out as she turned back around to admire the darkening sky, "Aaron has dreams too; I need to see what I can do to help him accomplish those. I'm thinkin' added income for the ranch might be nice. And the tractor, with the front blade for snow, I'd put that in the garage with my 4-wheel drive. I don't want it left outside anymore. Hey, this could help me get more organized, 'cause winter's coming. I'll talk with Granddad's former hired man, pay him for getting me oriented for winter, like figuring out how to start that tractor to plow to the highway, otherwise how'll I get to work in heavy snow?"

⁜

Julie watched the transformation of her cottage into a veterinary clinic. Julie's lawyer and accountant helped her work through the steps of becoming a landlord. Her insurance agent joined in to make the whole process happen. Aaron stopped by the cottage nearly every day to see the progress his contractor made. She learned that from the contractor. The last thing Julie did on her way home from her hospital shift was to stop and view the work Arch Bell did.

On a Tuesday in early November Julie arrived home before lunch with groceries for the week.

"I hate shopping; this'll do me until I do the big stuff for Thanksgiving."

She heard the doorbell, put one last item in the frig and headed for the front. She peeked into the security hole.

"Aaron, come in, it's been a while."

They stood silent, gazing at each other at the great room entrance. It zinged through Aaron's head again, "I want to wake up with this woman, every morning, for the rest of our lives."

Julie began to smile, looking at his left leg. The boot was gone, no cane either.

"Yeah, I was out on a call, had to put a horse down, hate when that happens, the owner just didn't have the heart to do it."

She watched his brown eyes shadow almost black and his lips thin.

"Wow, you're back to your old self, making calls out of the office. How's the foot?"

"Creeky, important that I step straight down on my foot, none of that putting weight on the outside of the foot, still sensitive, still got a little limp."

"Uh huh, it'll take a while."

"Julie, I've a couple of hours before my next appointment at the clinic. In some conversation with you, you told me you were off Sunday and Tuesday. Kinda spur of the moment, but hey, would you take a few minutes to look over the cottage (uh, almost the clinic) with me?"

"OK," he watched her nod and smile, "but truth be told, Aaron, I've been watching Arch and his crew, since they started working on the renovation."

"Ah ha, you've been doing some observing?"

"Yeah, but I haven't a clue what you plan to do with each room. The only thing I got involved in was the room addition on the back of the cottage."

They strode next to each other on the way to the construction. She turned her eyes toward him.

Her head spun, "Being with him's like with a grown-up Jace. I feel so comfortable, like we've been together in another place and time."

She shook her head.

"You OK? You were looking at me, but you were in a far off place."

"Yeah, that's right, I was."

Aaron showed her into the cottage/soon-to-be clinic.

She looked around, "Small waiting area?"

"Right, receptionist desk, will be here, I think."

"You're bringing your vet technician?"

"Absolutely, she'll still do all the duty plus phones. My bookkeeper will share the space with Christy; Melody's in the office Tuesday, Thursday, and Saturday morning. She becomes a sort of vet tech on Saturday mornings."

"Able to do a lot of different tasks."

"Yeah, that's right," he paused, "and the two gals love animals, so sympathetic to their injuries."

He continued his tour, showing her patient rooms, the expanded lab area and X-ray.

"So you've got a small public bathroom in the front and a private one back here. What's planned for the room addition on the back?"

"A small OR, the operating room in town just isn't sufficient, too cramped."

"When do you plan to move from town to here?"

"December 1, I'm not taking appointments that week, except absolute emergencies. My helpers have it all planned out; they're in charge of getting me moved, except the big stuff."

"Helpers are your vet tech and bookkeeper?"

"Yeah, awesome ladies, always asking for more things to help me with. I'm just so lucky that they stayed on after Doc retired. He really knew how to hire people who could do the job. For sure, I was the one who had to be retrained, to do things their way."

He laughed at what he just said. Julie joined in, giving him her wide smile.

"Wow, Aaron, it's really coming together, looks like Arch just has the final touches to do."

"I need to talk to Arch."

"Stay for lunch, I'm starving."

"Hey, I'd like that. See you back at the house?"

She nodded.

The soup boiled on the stove as Julie set out lunchmeat, cheeses, bread and lettuce so they could each make their own sandwich. She stirred the soup as the doorbell rang. She peeked through the security hole, a new item on her front door along with a new deadbolt. Julie felt safer once the door got fixed.

"Come in, come in, soup's on."

He gazed at her as she looked up into his eyes.

"Shimmering brown pools," he thought as he smiled to her.

"This's real nice of you, Julie."

She nodded as she showed him into the kitchen area where the sandwich makings were. He washed his hands with the anti-bacterial soap Julie kept at the kitchen sink. She poured out the soup, giving him the bigger bowl. He made himself a sandwich and a half. They sat next to each other at the long table Natalie Thurston left in the home for Julie.

"We hold hands for grace," she whispered to him. "Do you want to do grace?"

He nodded to her, held her warm hand in his and spoke a few words. They ate, not speaking but listening to a Garth Brooks CD.

Julie spoke up after the song concluded, "I like the *Last Dance* words. Hey, each day's so very precious."

"You can shout that out," he turned, smiling to her.

"Tell me stuff about you, Aaron."

"Then you'll tell me about Julie?"

She nodded to him as he began.

"I'll start from now back, been in Twin Trails since June of last year. I graduated from Cornell's Veterinary School."

"Wow, a top notch vet school."

"Right," he nodded as he turned to her. "I first decided where I wanted to be geographically as a vet; then I pursued four different vet situations. Doc Finnigan's was the best; he'd already built his client base. I'm simply stepping into his shoes, so to speak."

"Medical technologies, really advanced, and ramped up in vet medicine, like in people medicine."

"Yeah, unbelievable, one example is cancer vets uncover in an animal. Sometimes surgery is the simple answer."

"You're from?"

"Helena, Montana, my growing-up place. So Twin Trails, Idaho, is perfect, further south, wanta stay in the West."

"I'm an alum of Montana State; where'd you go for your undergraduate?"

"U. of Montana."

"I got a mountain of college debt," Julie paused, "no help from my family, so I'm chunking as much as I can each month into paying off my loan."

"Me, my family helped with my undergraduate; they said I was on my own with vet school, so I'm like you, a mountain of debt. The good news is my practice is flourishing, growing as a matter of fact, 'cause I get out to ranches and farms further away than Doc would go. So I'm payin' vet school debt. I'd saved enough during my first year of practice to almost totally pay for all the stuff involved in my new clinic. I kept my old truck and live in a tiny place. More than a few nights I've slept at the clinic when we had a difficult case. I'm so excited to get going."

He touched her hand, "That's thanks to you for visualizing my dream. Soon I'll be practicing just down the lane from you."

She put her hand on top of his, "Your eyes shine, happy eyes," she nodded to him.

"'Nough about me, what about Julie?"

She poured them more coffee and took away the dirty plates.

"Want your blueberry muffins warmed up?"

"Sure, thanks."

Aaron ate his way through two blueberry muffins smothered in butter as she talked about herself. She spoke of her life as Aaron had, from that day back.

"Brave, determined, you got a heck of a lot of initiative, that's how I'd describe you, Julie. What an incredible story. Uh, gonna make a judgement call, your parents had some streaks of irresponsibility."

"Right about that, but I no longer judge them, did the best they could given their circumstances, married at 18, me at 19, and no training past high school. Dad started at the casino in deliveries; he's worked his way up to casino cage manager, they saw how smart he was."

"Wow, that is something, and your mom got her CNA."

"Never thought about my parents, them having hopes and dreams; I was super insensitive to that at the time, just mad 'cause I took over for mom. Hey, I've invited my dad, brother and sister to Thanksgiving dinner here. They're coming along with Grandma Natalie and to spend the night. I didn't even invite my family to my graduation, isn't that awful?"

Their brown eyes caught and held, "Can't judge that one, sounds like you're working on reconciliation."

She nodded, "I kinda did reconcile with my mom last Christmas."

"It makes you happier, to mend those hurts in your heart?"

She heard the kind tone of his voice.

"It does; God's been right here, with me, every step of the way, urging me forward, to my next humble task."

Aaron shook his head. She saw his raised eyebrows. So she shared her story of Helen Keller moving from humble tasks to great tasks, as Julie was doing now.

"My granddad and I talked about Helen as we mended fences that last summer I visited. I used to come here as a child and later as a teen. I've always loved my grandparents' place, now mine."

She moved her hands above and around her and pointed outside the front window at the view of the long stretch of front yard. He watched her fold her hands over her heart.

"I feel love, ooohhh wow, the vibrations of love from the generations of Thurston's who've lived here, whose spirits are still within this home."

He touched her upper arm, "That'll continue, Julie, in your capable hands."

Julie rose to gather the dishes and cups from the table.

"Let me help you with these."

They loaded the dishwasher, and he walked with her to the front door.

"Take care."

"Know I'll see you around."

He smiled down to her, "Guaranteed, thank you, lunch was delicious."

Julie blew out a breath as soon as the door closed. A sexual jolt like a bursting ember hit her in her groin. She blew out another breath, "Oh my, my body knows what it wants, but where's my heart?"

§

"Ready for our walk outside for a while?"

Everyone joined in to enjoy the cloudless sky and the mild temperature for this Thanksgiving Day. After they all walked down the lane to the highway and back, Rich produced a football and a game began in the front yard. Natalie, Julie, and Amy took on Rich, Derek, and Aaron. Aaron arrived in time for pumpkin pie and was urged to help out. The guys were short one team member.

"Gotta give the girls a handicap."

"Hey," Amy stood tall and gave her dad the look, "just one point, us girls can stand up for ourselves."

"Deal," they gave each other a high five.

The game ended up being close. Everyone remained careful not to rough up Grandma Natalie too much. In one of the last plays of the game Julie missed a catch from Amy. She landed kerplunk, scraping her right cheek and the inside of her hand. The call from the guys' team went out for a doctor in the vicinity. Aaron fit the bill so they all trudged back inside for more pie and to watch the doc clean up the injured player.

"Looks like you might have a bit of a black eye."

She looked up at Aaron as he washed her cheek, "By golly gosh, I sure earned it."

They heard applause coming from the players eating pie at the table.

Aaron scrubbed the inside of her right hand with the antibacterial soap.

"A touch of ointment, this small bandage, you'll be as good as new in no time."

He smiled to her as he also applied a tiny amount of ointment to her cheek.

"Come eat pie," the crew at the table spoke out.

Because Julie was the injured player, they gave her two dobs of whipped cream on her pumpkin pie. Grandma Natalie and Aaron said their goodbyes. After that Julie walked everyone down to the cottage to show them the clinic from the outside windows. She described what would happen with each room and with the room addition at the back of the cottage.

"Wasn't this where folks came to get registered for hunting? Derek asked.

"Exactly, folks spent the night here, bedrooms, with two small bathrooms, tiny kitchen to get up and get going for early hunting. Plus the hunting guides often bunked in here, before heading out with a group."

As they left they saw the two signs leaning against the side of the cottage. In a few days the sign people would be out to install them in the ground. Aaron's clinic would soon open.

Back at the ranch home Derek picked up the dusty guitar which sat in its stand in the great room.

"Would you play for us, please Julie?"

Rich and his kids sat on the rug in front of the fireplace with its logs burning. Julie sat a little away from them and strummed several songs they all knew from their early days. She moved her eyes from the group to the front window with the setting sun splaying streams of pink, lavender, and orange at the horizon. She picked the melody of a song she wrote several years ago and sang along starting with the second time she played it. Soon the family had the words and joined in with the chorus. They clapped and cheered as she finished.

"This is a special Thanksgiving with you all here; thanks for coming."

Amy saw the fresh tears in Julie's eyes.

"It was our pleasure, your tears?"

"Happy tears," Julie smiled. "I played once in a while at a couple of places in Brakerman while I was in school, kinda a break from studying, really glad I kept it up."

"So are we, Julie," Rich smiled to her, "this is a special time for us all."

℘

"I can't help with this effort this holiday season. I'm working only part time."

"That was her conversation, just that."

Julie sat with her Director of Nursing in her office.

"Our hospital staff person, in charge of philanthropy, has sick parents."

"So who'll step up to take the effort over?" Julie asked Rosalie Turner.

"Our boss asked me to assign the task; it's our serious hospital commitment to the United Way every Christmas. Many civic groups contribute to United Way for this effort. I'm asking you to take on this task, Julie."

Julie took a deep breath and gave her a positive "Tell me what you need me to do."

"Many of the churches in Twin Trails do special holiday things, like adopting families within the congregation who have families in need. But smaller churches don't have funds available, or big enough congregations to help. And there are lots of hurting families who do not have a church family. They do use Food Bank."

"So I need to search out the neediest, those who fall through the cracks." "Julie, we've been failing to catch the neediest, and we must rectify that. Our county United Way will assist with the gift baskets, but we need names, addresses, and phone numbers, church affiliation if they choose to put it down, and needs. The list of names they have is not accurate. Unfortunately these folks are often on the move. I've contacted the Food Bank, and 211. You will need to get with them to identify these hurting folks who have no church backup or who live in temporary situations;

we have many invisibles. There are lots of struggling folks in our community."

"And by when does United Way need accurate, updated information?"

"If we can get names to them by December 12, that will be 12 days for them to get Christmas baskets to these folks. They'd like to have all the deliveries finished by December 24."

"I personally know of a couple of situations, from their ER visits. Would I be interfering if I contacted the elementary schools? It might be the only place we could identify our homeless population, or seriously hurting families."

"Goodness, I hadn't even thought about children's parents, we for sure have them in our community. And Julie, on your days here, you can take lunch from 12 to 12:30. Then you'll be in charge of this effort from 12:30 until 3 when your shift ends. I've already checked in with your immediate supervisor; she's totally understanding."

"You know I'll be out of the office a lot at 211 and Food Bank, the schools, and the churches. I'll be getting names, right?"

"Correct."

"Is there a computer in the administration office I can use to create an Excel spreadsheet for United Way?"

To herself Julie thought she absolutely would need to make at least two back up flash drives, keeping one at home, just in case the computer crashed at some point in the project.

"Of course, I'm letting you use Tami's computer, printer and desk; she'll be out afternoons in the admin office."

"Oh, Rosalie, for sure I'll follow through with United Way to make certain we compare our lists and delete inaccurate information. The worst nightmare would be to try and deliver baskets to wrong folks or wrong addresses. And just a final thought, I'll get with ministers in several small congregations I know about, to see what their families' needs are." She paused and shook her head, "Gosh we may need to even help a minister and his family.

They're so dependent on the folks in their congregations, many with just a small stipend from their higher church administration. I imagine a few of them also work full time jobs."

Julie saw a smile begin to form on Rosalie's serious face.

"I knew I could count on you, Julie. I know a little about your background, so you certainly understand about some of our families in Twin Trails. You'll start tomorrow, and I don't want you working on this project on Sunday or Tuesday. Your days off are your days off. You need that break from your busy shift."

6

Aaron opened the clinic door and brought in his bag and equipment from the birthing at the Rochester ranch. He took off his shirt and washed up in the sink off the operating room. He scrubbed his arms high up into his armpits. Using the fingernail brush he cleaned and cleaned, removing the last bits of blood and tissue from beneath his fingernails. He felt a queasiness in his stomach and remembered the box of candy one patient's family brought. Opening the frig he picked three pieces of dark chocolate from the gift box. He ate them, one right after another. He gazed at his watch, no food since lunch. The family wanted him to stay and eat after the baby horse came. But he looked at the sky, saw the clouds and decided the snow might be headed his way. As soon as he could, he headed away from the ranch.

He lay down, feeling the biting strain in his shoulders and arm muscles from helping the horse give birth. A blanket over him, one under him and a jacket rolled up for a pillow made up his bed.

"My helpers can wash up and sterilize the equipment, in the morning," he mumbled as he started to fall asleep.

Aaron started to rouse, hearing a knocking, opening his eyes to bright sunshine pouring into the front area of the clinic. The knocking continued. He got up in slow fashion, rubbing his face and running his hand through his unruly hair.

"Julie!"

"I noticed your truck parked here when I got up very early."

"Come in."

"You slept here, ouch, that's a hard floor."

He saw her smile and a note of sympathy in her voice.

"Yeah, it was so late when I got back from the ranch, was totally exhausted, so I crashed here."

He watched her pour coffee from the thermos into a cup.

"You need this."

"Yeah, thanks," he said as he sipped the hot stuff.

"Blueberry muffins, I figured you'd eat them."

"Uh huh, starving, thanks Julie, I see you're nurse-dressed. Have a good day at the hospital."

"I will, hope your day's not too jammed up."

"Thank you for being so considerate, hug?"

"'Course," she smiled as she stepped into his arms.

She felt the strength in his shoulders and arms as they hugged. She held on for a long time. In slow motion they let go of each other. As she stepped back from him, she kept her wide smile. She watched his smile back to her.

"Bye."

He stood there in a kind of stupor as she let herself out, her ponytail with its red ribbon swinging, empty thermos tucked into her arm. He shook his head.

"Is she my beautiful beloved? I once was so sure about another," he paused, "time Aaron, time."

He nodded his head as he scrambled to begin his day after he finished the last bite of his second muffin.

℘

"This has been such an interesting project. I've talked with elementary school principals and at least six ministers."

Julie met for the last time with the United Way Coordinator in charge of gift baskets for needy families in Twin Trails.

"You had so many additions for us, for our master list. We took a number of names off the list, people who we believe no longer live in our area. We certainly tried to contact them, via cell or emergency contact. I think we have a manageable list," Marcia nodded to Julie. "Are you satisfied with the master list?"

"I am, but I warn you that whoever helps you next year will need to do kind of the same procedures, expecting that there will be lots of changes."

"Right, folks move around a lot. I appreciate the flash drive and the hard copy of the list you gave us, plus your written suggestions about how to approach this process next holiday season. I thank you for all your hard work, and, of course, I've already notified the hospital of your outstanding effort via the letter I mailed yesterday. Are you happy to be getting back to being at the hospital for your whole shift every day?"

"I am, but this sure has been a revelation into how blessed I am; we all are, 'cause some folks have it so rough. The best thing they can do is keep sending their children to school, to somehow break the bonds of poverty. I've learned that education is the only future bright light for some of the children in these families. I know I really didn't appreciate what my parents were trying to do for my brother and sister and me, when we were younger."

Marcia smiled to Julie and nodded, "I didn't appreciate either."

Julie carried the warm glow of working on that project with her for almost a week after she returned to the hospital on full shifts. She observed her patients with a different awareness, with more compassion after talking to the ministers in the small churches. The stories from the schools made her absolutely shudder. That's where she found the families in the worst circumstances, those most in need of the gift certificates the United Way would provide. She only prayed the parents would use the certificates for the benefit of their children.

&

Julie filled in for a missing nurse in ER on that Friday. A father brought in the little boy, beaten up by his drunk mother while the father worked a temporary job. She recognized the name from talking with the principal at one of the elementary schools she visited to get United Way information. The principal got alerted by the first grader's teacher. And sure enough Julie found out by asking the father a few questions away from his son in the ER. He admitted they got a gift basket from United Way.

"We were so thankful for getting the basket. But my wife drank away one of the certificates. I felt so sick about that because she gets so mean and starts beating on my boy."

Julie felt stunned, a knife turning in her stomach. Her nursing supervisor called Child Protective Services, and they came, taking the child away from the father, and the home. She took a break in the nursing lounge after she finished up her computer work on the case.

"The poor little boy, what kinda chance is he gonna have?" Julie whispered as she tasted the bile rising up to her throat. She strode to the bathroom and vomited.

"Did I do the right thing, by helping out that nonprofit? Sometimes I question why I try to help, does it do any good?"

She called Grandma Natalie when her shift ended. Julie asked if she could come over and talk to her. Julie broke down as soon as her grandma opened the front door.

"Why do bad things happen to little kids?"

They stood together, and Natalie held her until her sobs subsided.

"Coffee and oatmeal cookies, come to the table, Julie."

They sat together as Julie cobbled the story together and sipped coffee. She ate an oatmeal cookie as she proceeded.

Natalie looked into her granddaughter's brown eyes, "We don't know why God does what he does. It's a mystery, but, granddaughter, what's important is right now for the little boy. What now, well, he'll go into a foster home, where his mother can't beat up on him. The little boy is already scarred from what's happened. What's best for the little boy, that's what everyone'll be concerned about. That's my fervent prayer."

Julie nodded her head, trying to make sense of what her grandma just said.

"You're a very sensitive nurse, tuned in to the emotional state of every patient. With some time you'll not get so upset, it'll get more routine."

Julie's forehead wrinkled as she looked at Natalie, "Hope I don't become too desensitized by all the bad I see."

She watched her grandma's nodding head, "You care a lot, Julie, and given your background, well, you'll always be able to call on God. He'll guide you through rough waters."

৪১

Julie read the ad in the Twin Trails paper.

"This is something to take little kids' minds off the big day coming up. I'm gonna dig out my old teddy bear with the nearly missing ear and take it."

She sat with several nurses on lunch break as she explained the information she read in the ad. Several of them confirmed what she read.

"My little boy's going. My husband's taking him 'cause I'll be here at work. How do you like working surgical by now, Julie?"

"So much, for the most part it's such a positive place, with people improving a lot after their surgeries. It's sort'a like Orthopedics, but I like Surgery better."

∛

Dr. Engleman held a Teddy Bear hospital where young children could visit the clinic and have their stuffed animal examined and helped. The idea came from one of his assistants whose young daughter wanted to be a veterinarian when she grew up. The second Saturday in December dawned cold with the promise of bright sunshine through the day. The Open House hours were 9 to noon. Each child and their injured stuffed animal were shown through the facility to the back so they could see the operating room. All the parents wanted to see too.

The response overwhelmed Aaron and the staff. By 10 they had helped 25 stuffed animals and their little owners. Julie stood in line inside the clinic. Behind her she saw the line snaking out to the opening of the lane. Cars were parked on the sides of the road clear up to her home. One assistant called out a name nearly every five minutes so the process moved along.

"Well hello young lady."

Julie handed her scruffy beat-up teddy bear to Aaron. She pointed to his right ear, almost detached from the rest of the teddy bear.

"And what is your name, young bear?"

"Little Bear," Julie answered as she smiled to Aaron.

In a swift motion Aaron attached a bright green band aid to one side of Little Bear's ear and a bright red band aid to the other side.

"Little Bear probably should have stitches, but this'll do for a while."

"Thank you, Dr. Engleman, I think Little Bear feels better already."

She shook hands with the veterinarian. He watched her smile up to him.

"This was so fun, wonderful for the children."

He nodded and escorted Julie and Little Bear to the hallway.

"Take care, Julie."

She nodded, and Little Bear gave a wave of his arm.

Like Little Bear each stuffed animal got a colorful bandage in the appropriate body location, and the child received an animal sticker for bringing the injured animal in. At 11:45 the line was gone and the doctor and his helpers started making order for appointments on Monday morning.

"Fabulous, that was so, so" he paused, "a blast; I hope the little kids had a good time. I sure did."

His helpers watched his wide grin.

"Aaron, it's a great way to introduce young people to a different kind of doctoring. Many of them have pets at home, and a few had already been in with a parent to take care of a sick animal."

"I agree. How many children did we welcome?"

Melody looked over the sheets of paper and added up the two pages of names.

"85."

"Oh my gosh," Aaron sat down in a chair in the reception area. "Do you realize what a great marketing tool that was?"

"Uh huh, maybe do this every other year, the children certainly enjoyed it."

"Maybe one day there'll be a vet from this group of kids."

"My daughter," Christy spoke up.

Aaron watched her nod to him, "She's more excited than ever after visiting today. She's always asking me to explain different procedures that I do. We've given her every horse story we can find in bookstores, and she keeps searching on her weekly trips to the library for all sorts of animal stories."

"Thank you ladies, an awesome effort today, as always."

They watched his smile and heard the appreciative tone of his voice. He hugged each of them as they got their coats and started to leave.

"Doc, you got Christmas plans?"

He shook his head, "Holidays are tough for us medical folks; I plan to stick around. Remember that I'm also covering emergencies for the vet over in Chocta County. He's got a young family and wants to spend time with them. There're quieter times, like in late January and early February, before cow birthings, I'll plan to head up to ski, haven't done that for a while."

℘

Julie worked five days straight and had two more to go. One day she pulled a double shift, 7 a.m. to 11 p.m. On Christmas Eve Julie agreed she would sleep over at Grandma Natalie's so they could be together for Christmas Day after Julie's shift.

"I'm exhausted, Grandma Natalie, from working that double shift. I went home to shower and gather clothes for work and here tomorrow."

They hugged after Julie made her statement.

"You just take it easy. I'll hang your clothes up in the guest bedroom and then put the presents under the tree."

Julie fixed herself hot chocolate and sat at the breakfast nook, putting her face into the steam coming off the hot chocolate. She took deep breaths of the chocolatey smell. As she sipped her drink, she let the activities of her busy day slide across her mind and flit away. She replaced them with prayer, for her family, herself, and her community.

Julie gazed at her grandma as she sat down with her hot coffee, "I love what you've done to your home, Grandma, the lightest of light blue walls all over, giving an illusion of the area being much bigger than it is. With the light gray carpet throughout, well, there's a calmness about the whole place, just like you're calm."

"Sure do like the carpet for its warmth on my sometimes bare toesies, easier to take care of than hardwoods."

Julie nodded, "I'm lucky in that it's just me at the ranch; the hardwoods, having them redone lighter, they're pretty easy for me."

"Honey, lie down. We're having soup and sandwiches for supper. We'll have a little something after midnight mass, too."

"Call me at 7?"

"I will, now go."

Julie lay down on the bed in the smaller of the two guest bedrooms. The walls in her room were the same color as the other two bedrooms, a tiny tinge of lavender. She remembered the guest bedrooms when she visited the ranch. Her grandma definitely chose a feminine look to her new home, not the rough and tumble beige out at the ranch. She realized that her grandma had all the ranch rooms painted an eggshell white when the renovation took place.

"Julie, supper," she heard her grandma's voice at her door.

"Thanks, I'm coming."

Joy to the World came to her as she brushed her hair for the meal. She hummed the melody as she helped her grandma set the table and bring over the food. They sat at the small table at the breakfast nook as they ate their vegetable soup and pb&j's. In the background she heard the Mormon Tabernacle Choir singing Christmas carols.

"Did you ever get to see the Choir, Grandma?"

"Only on television, but I'm told they really rouse an audience."

"Oh, my gosh," Julie paused, "they can really sing, and the sheer numbers of them, what a commitment of time and energy, and they're known all over the world."

Natalie nodded to her granddaughter, "That's for sure."

"The soup is uber delicious, you made it?"

"Nope, from a can; I don't cook much, just for myself."

"For dessert?"

"Knew you'd ask, with our decaf we'll have chocolate chip bars."

She watched her granddaughter's brown eyes widen.

"Yeah, so awesome Grandma."

෨

"Shute, I may not even get to midnight mass," Aaron spoke out as he headed out on an emergency call. The dog got into chocolate candy. He heard little children crying as he arrived in the kitchen. The family huddled near the dog, dad, mom, and three children, who appeared to be close in age, about 4 to 6.

The mother took the children away, and the dad helped Aaron clean up the dog, who sat in vomit and poop.

"Chocolate can kill animals."

"Yeah, we explained that to the children; it's been a good lesson for us all to keep all people food away from our dog."

Within an hour Milfurd started feeling better, with the hydration and medication Aaron gave him. The wife returned and heard the good news which she took back to the children. Calm returned to the home. Aaron left with strong words of caution for the parents. The next time they might not be so lucky.

He groaned as he saw cars jammed in the parking lots and along the streets by the church.

"I'll not be able to find a place to sit," he shook his head as he moved up the steps into St. Christopher's.

Julie sat on the aisle with her grandma next to her. She looked over to see a tall man in brown cowboy boots standing in the aisle, trying to figure out where to sit. She touched his arm and smiled up to him.

"OK?"

Julie and Natalie squeezed together, and Aaron joined them in the now crowded pew.

He knelt in prayer and then sat down.

"Thank you," he whispered to her, "I had an emergency, didn't think I would make it."

Father McMurray gave a short sermon. He knew the throngs of the congregation wanted to take communion. When the time came, Julie and Natalie sat, while Aaron and the rest of the folks in that pew got in line for communion.

"Oh gosh," Julie thought, "I certainly stand out as someone newer, who hasn't yet done the work to join."

ℰℴ

"She's beautiful," Lucas whispered as he came back from receiving communion. He sat two rows in back of the attractive blonde lady and her blonde companion, noting that they did not rise for communion. He got another glimpse of the lovely young woman before he knelt down in prayer for the communion bread he just received.

When he finished he sat and asked himself from where he knew that family. The blonde lady he was pretty certain, was Natalie Thurston. He remembered his dad bought a bunch of the Thurston ranch land.

"So who's the beautiful girl? They have the same color hair, not a daughter?"

He thought the Thurston's had two sons, who he saw from time to time growing up on the next ranch.

"It's gotta be a granddaughter. I seem to remember something, uh, let it go for now. But I'd sure like to meet that young lady. I'll check with mom."

He turned to look down to the white-haired woman who stood next to him, his mom. He shook his head as his mind spun out over all the events since his dad passed on.

ℰℴ

Julie felt her skin prickle as the church darkened. She looked around as the congregation lit candles, from one person to the next, until the whole church bathed in candlelight. Burning tears filled her eyes, as she sang the glorious *Silent Night.* Her grandma put her arm around Julie's waist as she put her arm around her grandma's shoulder. They held on tight while the next several stanzas of the song echoed throughout the church. Aaron stood next to them, sensing God as he rarely had, holding Aaron in His steady presence.

They stood among the crowd of folks leaving the service.

"Merry Christmas, Aaron."

"And Merry Christmas to you, Julie."

Natalie offered her hand, "I'm Julie's grandma, Natalie Thurston. She and I are headed home for special sticky pecan rolls, coffee and hot chocolate. Would you like to join us? Julie's got a short night, back on duty at 7."

"That would be really special."

Natalie gave him her address and directions to her home, not far away.

As Aaron drove he spoke out, "Last Christmas was super lonely; this will be nice, at least for a little while."

He smiled to himself as he walked up to the Thurston home. Julie met him at the door.

"Come in, come in, oh Happy Holidays, Aaron."

He watched her smile to him and heard a happy tone in her voice.

"I'll take your coat, Grandma Natalie in there."

Julie pointed in the direction of the kitchen.

"She's got yummy stuff for us to eat."

"Hi again, Mrs. Thurston, and thanks for the invite; this looks so good." He noted the sticky buns, cinnamon rolls, and especially the chocolate fudge displayed at the table.

"Decaf coffee?"

"Yes, please."

The three of them sat at the round table in the breakfast nook area and chowed down.

"This all tastes fabulous; reminds me of my mom when she gets a hankering to bake at the holidays."

"I'm sorry you'll not see your family this season, Aaron."

"It's for the best; truth be told I have several reasons for not going back home for the holidays."

"Wanta share?" Julie asked.

"Yeah, well I'm strong enough to tell it now; time heals."

Natalie nodded, smiling to Aaron.

"Dated a young lady through most of high school; we went our separate ways but unexpectedly found ourselves back at Cornell for vet school."

He blew out a big breath and shook his head.

"We lost touch and were shocked to discover we both wanted veterinary medicine. We dated at Cornell."

He stopped talking and drank the rest of his coffee.

"We were so much in love," Aaron looked up and out to the Christmas tree. He stopped talking.

"You don't have to go on, Aaron," Natalie spoke in a gentle tone.

"It's OK; I need to tell this." He moved his eyes from Natalie to Julie. "I was raring to get my practice started. She wanted to do Peace Corp. So we broke it off; it was rough going for about nine months, but gradually my practice became my life. I'm happy now. She's doing fine where she is, a lot of medical and educational stuff. But she's coming home to Helena for a short stay (a sick parent), so I'm not going up."

His eyes moved from Julie to her grandma.

"Thanks for listening; folks don't know much about me, I'm pretty private."

"Aaron, sounds like it was the right person, but the wrong time."

"Yeah, that's for sure, Natalie."

"My first love, high school, like you," Julie looked into Aaron's brown eyes, "I moved on to Montana for college after doing some nanny time. He had a two-year mission, uh, Mormon mission he wanted to serve after high school and before college."

"And you're happy now, being a nurse at the medical center?"

"Very, and having my own home, a year ago now I got ready to do my internship in Idaho. Unbelievable what can happen in a year."

"You'll be with friends tomorrow?"

"Yes, my vet tech invited me and our accounting person and her family for dinner Christmas day. The two of them are close, and they accepted me, kinda a younger brother, wow," he shook his head, "I've learned so much from them."

Natalie smiled to him, "The teddy bear hospital, that was their idea?

"Yeah, and it turned out great; Julie brought a teddy that need some ear work."

Julie laughed, "It was a lot of fun, oh my gosh."

Aaron glanced at his watch; it was 1:30 a.m.

"You gotta sleep; it's a wonderful Christmas Day for me already," he said as he smiled to them both.

Aaron hugged Natalie and then Julie as he left.

"Julie, I'll clear; you've got to get some sleep."

"Open presents when I get home from my shift?"

"Yes, let's."

෨

Julie struggled the next morning, trying to wake up from the few hours of sleep. She dressed in a quick hurry and went to the kitchen to make coffee. Her grandma had everything ready, so Julie just poured the water in the pot. When she came back out after brushing her hair and dotting on a bit of makeup, she stood in the kitchen.

"Thank you God for my life, for wonderful coffee, and Christmas mornings," she whispered.

When Julie got home from work, they opened the several presents in front of the glowing Christmas tree, with its white lights, gold and silver bulbs. Natalie's guest arrived shortly before the 5 o'clock dinner. Julie and Natalie both wore festive red sweaters and black slacks. Natalie made introductions and the three women gathered together in the kitchen. Julie poured white wine for the three of them and they toasted the holiday and the hope for the future year.

"Ham, Grandma, smells delicious, a bit of brown sugar and syrup over the top?"

"That's it."

"Well, everything smells wonderful, the fresh baked rolls," Cassie McCasland nodded her head.

"Cassie and I were neighbors, Julie."

She looked from one woman to the next.

"Our ranches, adjacent to each other."

"Gosh, was it your family that bought up a lot of the Thurston ranch?"

"That was us, Julie."

"So your family and I, well I'm your neighbor now."

"Right."

"What you did, Grandma, the selling, it's helped out the rest of the Thurston family so much. What a wonderful gift I've gotten, this year from you, a home of my own. I am so blessed," she hugged her grandma as tears came to her eyes.

Natalie started to cry, shaking her head, "Oh, Cassie, these are happy tears."

The women ate hearty, with a salad of many fresh vegetables, along with small red baked potatoes, the ham, and rolls.

"You said dessert was a treat, Cassie. What did you bring?"

"Cherry pie which I'll heat and then add a little bit of vanilla ice cream."

"Tell Julie about yourself, so she has a perspective on her next door neighbor family."

Cassie smiled as she began, "My husband died a few months after our family bought your grandparents' property. So Natalie and I share widowhood. We had three children, Gene and I. They all left the ranch and our community to go away to college. Lucas is retired from the Army as a major. Abby and Angie live a few blocks from each other in Boise. They're both teachers, married, and they each have two sons. Like your grandma, I moved from the ranch and bought a home in town. I wanted a different life, once Gene was gone. Natalie and I are both paraprofessionals, at different elementary schools here in Twin Trails."

"Oh my gosh Cassie, what about the ranch; it's huge now, the hunting operation?"

"Let's clear and we'll take our pie and coffee to the living room, enjoy the fire," Natalie declared.

They sat in front of the fire, with their dessert and coffee.

"To answer your question about the ranch, well Lucas is taking it over. And that's another story."

"Please, Cassie, I ought to know a bit about my neighbor, Lucas, since you're in town now."

"Explain the back story, Cassie, she needs to know," Natalie smiled to Cassie.

"Right, I mentioned that Lucas is retired from the Army. Actually it's a disability medical retirement."

"What happened?"

"Roadside bomb, Afghanistan, 2008, left foot nearly gone, amputated below the knee."

Cassie stopped and took a sip of her coffee, "It's still harder to talk about than losing Gene, 'cause Lucas has his whole life ahead of him."

"His prosthetic?"

"Doing great; he doesn't even limp. Wouldn't know anything ever happened except when he wears shorts, swims really well."

"So the docs fixed him up good."

"Lucas's pleased, which makes us all happy."

"Cassie, gonna stick my neck out here; why aren't you with your kids for the holidays?"

"Daughters' sons, all sick with a bad strep; they told me to stay away; we were together at Thanksgiving."

"And Lucas?"

"Spending Christmas with a recently injured vet; they served together early on. Lucas is in Reno."

"So he's taking over your ranch."

"Yes, he's been at it for a year; likes it, does some consulting for a defense contractor. He's an m.e., uh, mechanical engineer by degree and training."

"And his family," Julie paused and shook her head to Cassie, "absolutely none of my business."

"That's OK, he's been engaged a couple of times, once in college, and then again a few months before his injury. It just didn't work out with either woman."

Julie smiled, "Trust me, there is a woman out there for him. It takes time, and being in the right place at the right time."

Cassie nodded her head, "Gosh Julie, Lucas tells me that at least once a week. Lots of folks continue to pray for him, like when the community learned that he had been injured. We're a really patriotic community, several dozen of our youngsters serve, including three gals."

"I'm finding that out, often our patriots are small town kids, many from rural communities. As part of my internship before I graduated, I served at the medical center at Mountain Home Air Force base and also at the hospital in Mountain Falls, Idaho. Pilots that I went out with, they were all from smaller communities. They were interested in nurses as wives," Julie laughed, "I was committed to Twin Trails, so that was the end of THAT."

Both Natalie and Cassie laughed with Julie, "We're glad to have you with us, here, Julie," her grandma nodded her head to her granddaughter.

"And I'm glad to be here, not dating anyone, just trying to get my life under control, six months now, both at the hospital and out at the ranch; unbelievable how hectic my real life now is, that internship was just a tiny introduction," she smiled to both women.

Natalie went on to explain Julie's helping with the United Way holiday basket project through the hospital.

"Thank you for helping out, it takes all of us to make things work here, to care of all folks, especially the impoverished," Cassie patted Julie's arm.

℘ᴖ

Two days later Julie called her grandma, "I have New Year's Eve day off. I gotta work the next day though, so I'll miss a bunch of the football games."

One other item that Julie took care off when she moved in was having cable installed in her home. She couldn't believe that her grandparents still used an antenna on the roof of the ranch home, giving them just a couple of stations to watch.

"I'm enjoying having cable, Grandma, the sports, movies, and shows I hadn't seen for a while."

"Julie, I have an invitation to read to you. It's from Cassie McCasland. She gave it to me after you left on Christmas night for your own home. She's restarting the potluck tradition her family had for years at the McCasland ranch on New Year's Eve. She didn't have it for two years as Gene declined, and then after he died. And she's inviting both of us. Your dad and I always went, such fun, with the food and the singing, reminiscing and dancing."

"Hey I'd like to join in; I didn't have plans for New Year's Eve. I'll need to leave by 12:30, 'cause I gotta be at the hospital at 7. Grandma, please thank Cassie and let her know."

"Will do, love you granddaughter."

"Love you too, Grandma."

∞

"Welcome Julie, mingle and introduce yourself to folks."

Cassie hugged her and showed her the way to the bedroom where coats were put. She wound her way through the crowd of folks standing and talking. She saw her grandma laughing with a tall white-haired man.

"Wow, Grandma, it's good to see you smiling," Julie said as she moved to her grandma. The two women looked at each other and started laughing.

"We're wearing the same colors, like at Christmas."

"But Grandma, you and I didn't discuss outfits."

"Red, that's a great color for your blonde good looks, ladies," the man said as he admired Cassie and then turned to Julie.

"Oh Julie, this is Mitch Sanderfer. He's handling the hunting business on the McCasland ranch, just as he did when the hunting property was Thurston land."

"You're Rich's daughter?"

"I am."

"Your grandma mentioned you now own what remains of the Thurston land, the homestead, and outbuildings."

"That's right, the family agreed I was the correct person to take over. I love the land, my home, and the work I do, nurse at the Med Center."

"Good luck with all that, Julie, a lot of responsibility for a young person," he smiled to her, "Ladies, let's get in line for some fine chow."

Cassie realized one thing as the food line started to form. She forgot grace. And she saw Julie nearby.

"Please, honey, could you say a few words for my wonderful crowd."

"Of course, Cassie."

She got everyone's attention, and Julie began.

In a strong, well-modulated voice she spoke out as she looked out over the crowd,

"Let's bow our heads and be thankful, here's from Ralph Waldo Emerson,

'For each new morning with its light,

For rest and shelter of the night,

For Health and Food

For Love and Friends,

For Everything Thy

Goodness sends.'

Amen."

Mitch, Natalie and Julie loaded their plates. Julie went back for drinks for them.

"Beer for you, Mitch, Grandma, white wine for you and me."

She set the drinks above the plates at the table.

"Thanks, sweetie."

An empty chair sat next to Julie at the large table.

"Mind if I join you folks?"

Julie turned to the low voice and looked up and up to a very tall, very short-haired blonde.

"Course, Lucas," Mitch said.

Once he got settled Julie realized that he knew Mitch and Natalie.

She turned again to him and offered her hand, "Hi, I'm Julie Thurston."

He took her hand in his large, rock hard hand and shook it firmly.

"Lucas McCasland."

"That's one serious hand used to hard work," Julie thought.

Julie looked at his piled-up plate and realized he didn't have a drink.

"I'm going for a glass of water; could I get you anything to drink?"

"Swell, beer would be great; that's real kind of you, Julie," he smiled to her and nodded.

She wound her way to get drinks and back again with a glass of water and a beer.

"Thanks."

The four of them ate in silence for a little while. Julie tried to recall what Cassie had said about her son. It simply didn't come to her. So much of the time she was trying to put names and faces and information together. It didn't matter, where ever she was as well as at the hospital.

"Information overload," she told herself.

Julie went for seconds and got pumpkin pie piled with whipped cream. She started in on the pumpkin pie.

"Uuummm, delicious, you three gotta try it."

"I did the pie," Lucas smiled as he shared.

"Where'd you learn how to cook, uh, bake?" Mitch asked.

"Always enjoyed it, learned watching mom bake in the kitchen."

"Admire your whole kitchen, so open concept, looking out to the great room with the wonderful stone fireplace, actually, Lucas, this looks like my kitchen."

"Good job, Julie," her grandma added, "actually Lucas used our designer and contractor to do his home."

"Yeah, back in the day, growing up in this home, it was so boxy, opened up a bunch of walls. It all works great now. It's my home now, barely recognize it from the way it was."

"It was a very good fall season for the hunting, Lucas," Mitch said.

"And according to you, next year will be better, right?"

"That's correct. You are plumb easy to work with, Lucas."

The guitar players started tuning up as some guests helped in the kitchen and others moved tables to the outside and put chairs and couches around in a circle so folks could dance. The players started out with several old country ballads for everyone who wanted to sing. Then Julie heard more modern country songs, including one of Blake Shelton's Christmas pieces. Julie gave her grandma a hug.

"Care to dance?"

"Very much," Julie looked up to Lucas and smiled.

He held out his hand to help her stand.

"I saw you at midnight mass with your grandma."

Lucas held her in his strong arms as they danced the two step in the small dance area. She looked up to him.

"You did?"

"I was two rows behind and to the side of you. I went with my mom. I saw you the second time as I came back from receiving communion. I decided then and there that I had to somehow meet you."

Julie nodded her head and smiled, "And here we are together."

"That's right, a wonderful gift to meet you on this last day of this year."

They fell silent as the song finished, just standing together in the middle of the floor, couples surrounding them.

"Care to dance one more?"

"Absolutely, I cannot remember the last time I danced, it's been ages, and I'm enjoying being with you," Julie felt her face flush red.

Lucas stepped back, "Is that a little blush I see on your face?"

Julie giggled, "Guilty."

They danced this slow dance and she felt his strong lead. She relaxed and melted in his arms.

"I would like to go out with you, Julie," he spoke in a soft tone to her.

She nodded to him as he led her back to an empty chair.

"I'd like that too; you've got hostessing to do. My home still has the land line."

"That's good to know; I'll be in touch, a happy New Year to you," he said as he smiled down to her.

"And a happy New Year to you, Lucas."

Julie mingled with the other guests, getting acquainted with some of her neighbors and several townspeople. She danced with a nice young man who saw her at the hospital. She got assigned to be his granddad's nurse after his granddad's surgery. Her grandma found her as midnight approached.

"Grandma, I gotta drive soon, so no champagne for me. You go ahead, have a sip."

At the stroke of midnight the guitarists started up *Auld Lang Sine* and everyone joined in singing. Julie and Natalie held hands.

"I wish you a wonderful New Year, Julie, and I am so glad you're here in Twin Trails."

"And I'm happy to be here; I never realized how wonderful it is to have a grandma."

Julie watched her grandma's brown eyes sparkle in the overhead light. Natalie saw the brown pools of her granddaughter's eyes.

They hugged, and Julie headed for her home.

ॐ

Julie got used to plowing her driveway during the snowy month of January.

"I'm getting good at running the old tractor with the blade," she would tell her patients as she tended to them in the surgical wing. Lots of patients had similar stories to tell her about their experiences plowing roads out in the Idaho countryside.

Julie and Lucas began having dinners together. Once a week Lucas would cook, and Julie would bring wine. The next week Julie would cook and Lucas would bring wine. They alternated like that until mid-February. They enjoyed the food, fun, and interesting stories of their previous lives.

"I'm still fighting PTSD, probably will be the rest of my life," he admitted to her as they sat in front of the fire at Julie's. They started to have their dessert.

"Let's stop and talk about what's going on with you, Lucas."

"Oh I'm getting help with my depression and such. Also I'm trying to invite more love into my life, but I'm finding it hard to date, in this small community, so many of the women are married, or divorced with kids."

He stopped talking and smiled to Julie.

"It's refreshing to communicate with someone who knows what's going on in the world, who's in the trenches fighting for the health of folks in our community. Nursing is such a worthy calling; wow, that was something to have their care after I got hurt. Angels, I think you all, you medical folks, are angels among us. Because of folks like you I am still alive today."

"Our calling, Lucas."

They stopped, drank their coffee and ate the apple cobbler Julie baked.

"This cobbler is so good, the cinnamon just right and the apples nicely cooked." He stopped, took a deep breath, "I'd like to continue to see you, Julie."

She turned and faced him, "To be honest with you, there is someone else I'm seeing now. I have decisions to make,

Lucas; they involve you and this other person. So I need to step back from you; please date others. You are a fine man."

She smiled, and he heard the soothing tone of her voice, "I am so grateful to you for your service to our country."

Julie saw the disappointment on his face, and something else she didn't expect, an anger shining in his eyes. Then her medical mind sifted through what he had been through. So she understood.

&

"A glorious few days of skiing, what do you think, Julie?"

"I'll get with the surgery scheduler to see if I could get a Monday and a Wednesday off; that would give me Sunday through Wednesday, a travel day on each end and two full days of skiing. Would that work, Aaron?"

"Ask, then I'll get my calendar coordinated. My buddy, he'll handle any emergencies."

They sat together on the large, L-shaped couch, getting ready to watch a movie. The pop and popcorn sat on the coffee table in front of them.

"For years now, Julie, I've wanted to do a several day ski trip, all through vet school, just a dream, but now I can actually swing it, and with you, babe."

They turned to each other and kissed, a long, slow, teasing tongue kiss. Julie felt the jerk of a hot sexual jolt in her groin. When their kiss ended she gave a little gasp.

"Hurts, doesn't it, the sexual feeling, I've got it with you, Julie."

"Yeah, it hurts like heck; I want you, I need you. I'm in love with you, Aaron," she touched her fingers to his cheek.

"Confession time."

He watched her eyes widen.

"Second time I saw you, at your home, with Joe, the realtor, when we worked on the new location for my clinic. I thought, I thought," he paused as Julie saw tears form in his eyes, he let out a deep breath, "my mind told me that I wanted to wake up with this woman (you) every morning for the rest of our lives."

He hugged her as they both struggled with tears and confusion in their thoughts.

She moved away from him in slow motion, "Oh my gosh, Aaron, oh wow."

He smiled to her, "Yes, oh wow," he nodded.

They snuggled in each other's arms as the movie began.

7

"Military Mountain, that's what they call this place, Julie, that's my surprise. You knew the what, just didn't know the where. I'm told the skiing's pretty awesome, but, we may even want to do a snowshoe one afternoon to view some of the winter wonderland and the amazing animal tracks in the snow."

Julie gazed around at the blueish white landscape, in the little valley as Aaron drove, up to the ski mountain. The resort rested at the mountain's base.

"I'm excited; it's after Valentine's Day so the lodge may not be so crowded."

"Yeah, and it's well before spring break time, not so many young people around."

"Hey, we're still part of the age group."

"Whew, I don't feel young, footloose and fancy free."

Julie paused, "Er, well neither do I. We got lots of responsibilities in our lives."

They checked in, taking separate one bedroom rooms a few doors from each other. Julie insisted. An hour later she heard the rat-tat-tat on her door.

"How's my afternoon ski buddy?"

Aaron gave her a huge grin; he watched her sparkling eyes.

"Ready to ski, please just a couple of hours for me," she nodded, "I've been doing my exercises faithfully. And you know how much I'm on my feet at the hospital."

Julie felt wobbly as she skied off the ramp and down into the people waiting to ski the hill. She held tight to her poles as she followed Aaron to a quieter area.

"Golly, gosh, it's been awhile, Aaron. I skied with the family when I was a nanny, up in Montana, but not really since then."

"I'll stay close by, you may want to ski just green this afternoon."

She smiled to him, "Just to let you know, I'll ski green the whole time I'm here. You go ahead on the blues when you feel comfortable. I know real clearly what I can do physically, and skill-wise."

"Got it, Julie."

He shuffled close to her and gave her shoulders a squeeze. They skied down and rode the lift back five times that afternoon.

"That's it for me, Aaron, I can meet you at the cafeteria area if you want to do one more run."

"Go ahead then, I'll do one blue hill and meet you inside. We can decide on what to do after that."

That evening they ate a leisurely dinner in the dining hall of the lodge.

"It's been a grand first day, Aaron."

"You're doing really well, Julie; you may even be able to master the parallel before you leave. It's just a matter of practice."

"I'm exhausted, Aaron, I need a good night's sleep; this altitude just knocks me out."

Aaron left her at her room. They stepped inside, hugged and kissed, another sensual tongue-teasing kiss. She felt an intense heat blowing through her.

"He feels it too."

As he walked down the hall to his own room, the urgency hit him.

"I want to date her, and care for her. I need to ask her if she'll continue to date the rancher. I want to know what she wants."

They hit the slopes by 9:30 on Monday morning. Julie watched the sun try to shine through the parting clouds and tiny bits of snow fall from the sky. They stopped at 12:30 and had soup and sandwiches in the ski lodge diner. Julie got hot chocolate for both of them after they drank a lot of water.

She returned with the two hot drinks. They sat close in the crowded eating area.

"Somethin's buggin' the heck out of me, Julie."

He turned toward her, "You been really honest with me, that you are also seeing another man. I guess I need to know your intentions, but I understand it's none of my business, your personal life."

Julie nodded to him, "I explained to the gentleman that I wanted to date another man (you) exclusively. We liked each other, but that was it for me. He really wants to get married. He's some older than us."

"Yeah, I understand from my assistants that he's a military hero, disabled."

"Right, several issues, uh serious."

"Uh huh, they also told me that."

"Come to my room tonight; we'll have some champagne to celebrate our successful ski day and one more ski day tomorrow."

They sat together in the dining room enjoying the prime rib and pecan pie.

"This is all so delicious, and yes, it would be fun to come to your room. Tomorrow night, I'll invite you to visit mine. I'll have a little special drink to fix for us. We have lots to talk about, our futures, what we want."

"Welcome to my abode, Julie."

They hugged. He held her hand and led her to the small circle table in the corner of his room. Julie noticed a bottle of opened champagne, a small box of chocolate cherries, and a single rose bud sat on the table. They sat close, pulling their chairs together. They toasted with champagne, ate several of the chocolate cherries, and each smelled the spicy odor of red rose bud.

They talked of their school days, especially their last year, when they started getting indoctrinated into the real world, of working with sick animals, their owners, helping sick humans and their families.

"We move people from health care to health, animals too."

"Right, oh Aaron I can feel the champagne; makes me giddy and wanting to dance," as they finished off the whole bottle.

Aaron found a radio station with danceable music. Julie stood next to him and started to dance around on her own. Aaron gathered her in his arms for a slow dance. She put her arms around his neck as they eased into each other. Aaron pulled her tight to him. Julie felt his hardened penis against her tummy. They danced in slow motion, around and around.

"Julie, I want to make love to you, but not like this, when we've had the champagne."

"Sober, sober, when we give ourselves to each other, Aaron."

"Right, take the rose."

"Keep the chocolates for the trip home."

They kissed and kissed, rousing them to a fever pitch, their groins on fire, aching. Aaron stepped back.

"We need to say goodnight, powerful, what's happening to us."

Julie nodded, hugging him and then stepping back.

"I'll meet you in the dining room for breakfast at 8, OK?"

"Perfect," Aaron nodded to her.

She watched his smile.

"He cares, he really cares," Julie thought as she walked down the hall to her room.

Aaron knelt by his bed, "God, I've found her; thank you for bringing her to me, unbelievable, just down the lane from each other."

℘

Julie and Aaron separated after the first run Tuesday morning. She took her time, practiced her parallels on the green trails. He moved to the blue trails. They met for lunch.

"Let's snowshoe this afternoon. It's more intimate; we can walk and talk."

They found the snowshoe trails to be wide and flat from the snowshoers who went on the trails earlier in the day. They walked along, side by side.

"Julie, I heard from my mom a few days ago. Dad's not feeling so good. They'll call me after they meet with the cardiac surgeon."

"You haven't told me about your family, especially their medical situations."

"MI for dad, four years ago, cleaned up his act, no more pipe, lost weight, started exercising. Mom and he eat better."

"On meds for the heart attack?"

"Yeah."

Julie put out her arm to stop him as she held on to both her poles with her other hand, "Damage has been done?"

She held on to his arm. He wore sunglasses as did she. So she couldn't tell what his eyes were telling her.

Aaron stood for a little while, not moving.

He turned to Julie, "Damage done," he nodded to her.

Julie felt her heart lurch, and she stepped closer to him.

"Aaron, each day is precious, go see your dad, while you still can."

"I need to, hey, Julie," he paused, "us too, we don't know what God's plan is for us. We're not invincible."

"Yeah, just human, and humble, and grateful for what we have."

"Right, you really know how to say it, Julie."

They decided on an early dinner, stuffed pork chops, salad, rolls, and a decadent chocolate brownie, covered in chocolate sauce, with whipped cream over all that.

"Only one glass of wine for me tonight," Julie nodded as she gave her order.

She eyed Aaron as he ordered just one glass. He remembered their conversation of last evening about being sober. They sat in front of the massive fireplace in the lodge, sipping decaf coffee.

"These days with you, perfect Julie."

She nodded to him, "For reals, we may never again have such a time of serenity, with the snow, the sky, just with each other."

They walked hand in hand to Julie's room.

"I'll be back in a few minutes, need to go to my room."

She kissed him, "See you," then she winked, causing them both to laugh.

When he came back, Julie had changed into soft baby doll pj's with pink bottoms.

"You turned the lights down; and I hear country sounds in the background, oh Julie."

They danced one song. She helped him undress.

"You're beautiful, Julie," he whispered as he helped her out of her pj's. He bent and kissed each of her nipples, then held her tight to him and cupped her buttocks into his hard calloused hands.

They kissed and caressed and moved to the bed together. A sexual ache roused Julie to a fever pitch. Aaron ached and ached for many days before this time with Julie.

Aaron mounted her as their kisses deepened. He felt the nod of her head as he entered her, slow, slow. They moaned together as Aaron moved his head next to hers. He raised up once to kiss her. The stroking began and then continued; he felt his orgasm coming, coming as she felt hers. They exploded together, the semen filling his rubber. He collapsed in her arms, and they held on to each other, not wanting to let go.

"This is what sex with love feels like," Julie told herself, "unbelievable."

"Julie, oh Julie," he whispered to her, "my beloved."

She whispered back, "My beloved."

An hour later they made love again, savoring the exploring they began with each other's bodies. After that they slept.

They stood in the shower together the next morning.

"I love being with you like this, Julie."

"Me, too," she replied as they soaped each other and rinsed each other off, the heat of the shower matching their rising heat for each other.

Later she hummed as they dressed together.

Silent Night?

"Yeah, I hum holiday songs all through the year, mostly Christmas. My patients get a big kick out of me, the Christmas kid."

"Wow, I didn't know that about you."

"Yeah, well we have to do a lot of exploring of each other. Just like, I didn't realize you would eat anything put in front of you."

"Right, I just don't like to cook, and I'm always hungry."

She kissed him soundly on the lips, "Like this morning, you polished off all the chocolates with cherries."

He stepped back from her, "Yeah, that's my appetizer before breakfast."

They laughed together and she hugged him again, "Let's get us starved folks down to breakfast. Skiing brings out big appetites."

He held her close before they left her room, "Making love to you also whets my appetite," he whispered.

She held him tight, then let go. They walked hand in hand to the dining room.

ↄ

All the way back to Twin Trails she kept her left hand on his right knee. They drank coffee and had donuts at the shop where they stopped, half way home.

He walked her to her front porch.

"I love you, Julie," he spoke in a solemn tone as he searched her brown eyes.

"And I love you, Aaron, one day at a time, we've so much living to do, so many more ski and snowshoe trips."

He nodded, picked her up and twirled her around. They hugged and she watched as he returned to his pickup. They waved to each other and smiled.

ॐ

The next two weeks Julie lost two patients in Surgical. Each time that happened Julie went through an inventory in her mind as to what happened. In each case, a secondary infection after the surgery caused the deaths. Everyone redoubled their efforts to keep infections at bay, staph, strep, C Diff, and MRSA. It was a constant struggle for everyone in the hospital community, from the housekeepers to the nurses who watched over the patients, to the doctors who did the surgeries and follow up situations.

ॐ

"I need your help, Julie."

She looked at her caller ID on her home phone. There was no name, and she did not recognize the phone number, probably cell.

"Who's this," Julie replied, trying not to sound irritated. She just got home from a hard day at the hospital. And she was hungry. When she got hungry, she got cranky.

"Lucas McCasland, Julie, I'm having a rough time right now. I thought about it, and I decided to call you. Can you come over and talk. You kinda know my story. I'm scared of what I'm doing."

"Sure, Lucas, you alone?"

"Yeah."

"At your ranch home?"

"Yeah."

Julie made a quick change into jeans and a turtleneck with a sweatshirt over. She grabbed a chocolate bar and water and headed out to the McCasland ranch. It was close as the crow flies, but took longer to head down the highway a mile and then down a lane, the lane a little bit further distance than her own. She also remembered a first aid kit she kept at home, just in case.

She found the front door unlocked. As she looked around she found the house to be in perfect order, a typical military situation, everything looking very squared away.

"Lucas, Lucas, are you here?"

Silent, she heard nothing. She started to go from room to room, looking in each of the guest bedrooms, and the guest bathroom. Julie saw a light on in the master bedroom. She noted the bed, made neat as a pin. She started to smell something, it was nauseating, as she edged closer to the master bathroom.

"Lucas, Lucas, are you in here?"

She opened the door a little more. The smell suffocated her; she stepped back, coughing and choking. She opened the door wide and saw him. The light from the bedroom was dim, but she saw his head bent over as he sat on the edge of the tub. She saw one hand hanging into the tub and a large hunting knife in his right hand. She turned on the light and gasped.

"Lucas, oh Lucas."

He raised his head to her, but his eyes were unseeing. He wore boxer shorts, and he had his prosthesis on. She laid the first aid kit on the sink counter.

"I need to take this from you, Lucas."

Gently she unfolded his fingers and took the hunting knife and put it on the floor away from him. She looked at his arm hanging into the tub. She shook her head as she noted the amount of blood already pooling in the tub. His cell phone sat in the middle of the pool. She pulled towels from the towel rack and cut them into strips with the knife. She wrapped the strips tightly around his lower arm, to slow the bleeding. She moved back and washed her hands so she could call 911. Julie made the call, then stepped against the sink and vomited.

Lucas covered himself with feces, on his face, down his chest, and all over his arms and hands. The stench overpowered her for a little bit. Then she got her bearings and using towels as gloves she helped ease him from the tub ledge to the floor of the bathroom.

"Lucas, help me, you're heavy."

He seemed to respond but still landed hard on the floor. She applied the tourniquet tighter to try to stench the flow. Julie stuffed towels under his cut arm.

"Julie, thanks, you're my angel," she heard his hoarse voice.

As she watched him stabilize, she realized that his home remained dark. "I gotta get some lights turned on inside."

She did a quick check of his respiration and pulse, then hurried through the home and remembered the front porch light for the EMT's.

She led the ambulance crew to Lucas with a warning of what they'd see.

"Unbelievable what we encounter, Julie," one of the EMT's shook his head.

"I'll meet you at the hospital, just want to make sure he's gonna make it,"

Julie felt numb as she parked in the emergency room lot. Her tummy started flipping as she entered the ER waiting room. Soon she looked in on Lucas. His mom stood next to his bed. When Cassie McCasland saw Julie, she rushed to her. They hugged.

"It's the PTSD; it's bad Julie. The staff said you were with him, saved his life, staved off the blood. He could'a died, if he hadn't called you. I'm so grateful."

"I'm a nurse, it helps," she stood back from Cassie, "that he called me. I'm going to the dining area for food. Join me if you want."

℘

Julie ate, savoring the ham and cheese sandwich and a fruit salad. She started in on her dessert of a tangy lemon bar when Cassie joined her.

"He'll go back into therapy; and back into his support group. He thought he was doing so well. But I guess there are setbacks."

Julie nodded her head to Cassie, "There are, and it's possible they'll continue. Get your coffee and something yummy and I'll stay on a bit."

They talked for a few minutes when Cassie returned. She told her that she understood completely about Julie stepping back from Lucas. Julie noticed that Cassie smiled as she made that statement. Julie needed to go home. She winced as her head continued to pound on the drive.

"It was another short night," she told herself as she heard her bare feet patter on the hardwood floor early the next morning. She moved about the kitchen making coffee, humming, and setting up the toaster to make waffles.

℘

"Can't do movie night with you, Julie, but I need to come over. Stuff's goin' on."

For several weeks after helping Lucas, Julie felt a little down, partly the cold and snow, and partly beginning to understand what might lie ahead for her.

"I want to be with Aaron, that's all I know now," she kept telling herself. She also confided that to her Grandma Natalie.

Julie and Aaron sat, drinking decaf coffee.

"Dad's real sick; I'm goin' back home to Helena; think it'll be surgery."

"Heart?"

"Yeah, remember I told you about the attack he had. I'm pretty upset, kinda disturbed about us."

"Explain," Julie directed her eyes to Aaron's.

"You been payin' attention to the PTSD guy, Julie. You and I, I thought we are a couple. I don't like it, what's goin' on."

"Hey, Aaron," she felt her anger rising and could feel the flush start on her face, "Le'me paint you a picture. I'm tryin' to help someone willing to sacrifice his life for his country, for me, for our freedoms. He's in rehab," she paused and shook her head, "I'm not gonna see him again. I just wanted to make sure he was headed in the right direction. What's happened to him, it's gonna stay with him for the rest of his life, his loss of his leg and the frightening aspects of PTSD."

Julie got up from the dining room table where they sat. She paced back and forth, and then stood, away from him, but still looking at him. She spoke in a louder voice.

"He was willing to give his life, oh, my gosh, Aaron. We're so spoiled; we sat at our universities, letting this whole conflict thing whiz by us, without a care in our tiny little collegiate worlds. I'm really angry with you; I'm glad you're headed back to be with your dad. That's where you belong."

She practically spat the words out.

"That's right, it is, Julie, and I think you and me, we need to take a break from each other."

Aaron watched her nod her head in agreement, a determined look shining in her eyes.

"Uh huh, you don't own me, Aaron, we got lots to work out, and time away from you, that's gonna be a good thing for me. I have a ways to go before I even have my first year in at the hospital. I gotta be sharp, on top of things, every minute of every hour there, for my patients."

"Hey, I feel the same way, on top of my game to take care of the sick animals. I'm not shirking responsibilities."

Julie slammed her hands flat on the table.

"Stop, we gotta stop, us using these kinds of words. I won't have any part of that. Please leave, Aaron; I'll keep your dad in my thoughts and prayers. God's in charge."

He stood up and shook his head, "Bye, Julie."

"Bye, Aaron."

She watched him grab his coat and put it on. He walked out the front door, not looking back. He closed the door, hard. Inside Julie blinked back tears coursing down her cheeks. Before he could drive away Aaron brushed away the tears trying to blind his eyes.

&)

"I don't understand," she spoke to the nurseryman before he started to unload the five foot spruce trees.

He had just finished creating the holes for the trees.

"There is so much beauty looking out over our countryside."

The nurseryman nodded.

"My grandparents just didn't see the possibilities, the beauty that could be in their own back yard."

Julie made a promise to herself that she would bring color and trees to her home. She felt satisfied with the trees and grassed-in front yard. Her grandparents let the ground in the side yards and back yard return to native grass. Once they had a garden in one section of the split rail fenced-in area. But that hadn't happened for a long time. This year the just-planted spruces and a flower bed with several rose bushes in back were her goals. She just didn't have time for any other outside projects.

She and her grandma made rapid progress in their desire to become Catholic. By September (it was May now) they would take all the steps necessary. Church attendance on Saturday eve or sometime Sunday became mandatory for them, just as it had been when they were part of the Mormon church. Church attendance was nothing new for either of them. They both wanted to help with volunteer efforts. Since Natalie worked part time, she got involved with the Women's group at church. They accomplished all sorts of efforts out in the Twin Trails community.

Julie could only volunteer on Tuesdays. She remained on the 7-3 day shift, with Sundays and Tuesdays off. It worked for her and for the surgery wing staff. A request came to the Catholic parish for help at the city library. Julie read to little children at a 10:30 a.m. story time on Tuesday mornings. She loved the prep work, sometimes creating a little dance to go with a story, or a song, or sometimes she would wear a funny appropriate hat.

"It makes me feel so good to see healthy children, ages three and four, with their wide eyes and their welcoming minds and hearts," she would tell their parents and the staff at the library. "I see and feel the sometimes not-so-healthy situations of my patients in Surgery. So I love the positive vibes I get from the kids in the reading circle."

℘

Aaron and Julie remained down the lane from each other. But they continued to be apart. Julie did not hear from him during the week he spent with his family in Helena. The only thing she learned was that Aaron's father did have heart surgery. Spring tried to come to the area, but snow continued to fall, alternating with warmer days, confounding even the meteorologists who wanted to start predicting warmer weather. Julie continued to check on Lucas with phone calls. He understood they could only be friends. And he accepted that. She felt positive about the progress he made. He spent time in a special out-patient wing of a VA hospital, a wing devoted to returnees from the conflict that was winding down in the Middle East.

"My job, with God's helping hand, having people return to good health," she repeated that dozens of times each day.

℘

In May Aaron called Julie.
    "It's good to hear your voice, Aaron."
    "And it's good to hear yours."
    "What's up?"
    "Dad died."
Julie took a deep breath and blew it out in slow motion.

"I'm so sorry, Aaron," she paused, shaking her head, "sad for you and your family. I heard he'd been doing well."

"That's right, but God needed to take him home."

"Want to talk about it?"

"Can't, heading back up to Helena; Mom's handling the funeral stuff. She and dad worked on this some time back, for this day that they knew would come."

"Anything I can do, to help you out?"

"Prayer, lots of it, for my family, for me, for us to cope with this new change in our world."

"Your parents still work, right?"

"Uh, huh both educators, so the good news is that the school year is nearly over, Mom will have this summer to grieve and heal."

"That's good."

"Oh Julie, one of my vet techs is driving up for the funeral, not sure which one."

"I'm glad; she'll kinda represent the Twin Trails community."

"Yeah," he paused, and Julie could tell from his faltering voice that he was starting to cry.

"Julie," he paused again, "besides praying for all of us, I would really like for you to come to Dad's funeral. I need to see you, right now, pretty desperately, want you to meet mom. I'm kinda nuts, this back and forth, seeing him sick, get better, then quick sick, and then dying. I wasn't there when he died."

"Aaron, I don't know, I'd check with my surgery supervisor, don't know what the work load is like for the next few days. If I can, I'll come, but it'll be last minute, uh, the decision."

He gave her the funeral date, and they said their goodbyes.

֎

"It won't be long now."

Julie giggled, "Oh Christy, I can tell you have kids; I know it's one of the things they always ask."

"That's right, but it's a real pleasure to ride along with another adult, a woman like you, a nurse. You've given me quite a few insights, some that I can use with my animal patients, and with their human parents."

They both laughed.

"I'll have just put in one year at the hospital next month. Believe me, I still have so much to learn."

"Same with the animals, I been at this a good while, with Doc Finnigan before Aaron. Every day something new comes along, the technology's forever changing. Aaron gets several journals, has us read some of the articles. It's hard to stay up to date."

"That's for sure; we have fairly constant retraining at the hospital, every few months, just to catch up."

&

Christy and Julie ate a big breakfast in the dining room of the hotel where they spent last night.

"We gotta eat hearty; I have no idea what to expect. Aaron's private; he never really spoke about his family."

"All he told me was that his parents were educators, that his mom would have this summer to work her loss."

They found their way to the graveyard. A private security firm helped with parking the enormous number of cars. It was a celebration of Mr. Henry (Hank) Engleman's life. As Julie walked toward the hundreds of people, she noticed something a little unusual about the crowd. Many were teens; cheerleaders had on bright red and black cheerleader outfits. Some young men wore football uniforms, others had basketball warmups, still other wore baseball uniforms, track, and cross country warmups. A small contingent of the band stood in their band uniforms, their instruments held in their hands. When the time came, they played *Amazing Grace.* She watched a large red flag with the high school name on it. The flag swirled around in the breeze.

"I imagine the family is under the small green tent, sitting in chairs,"

Christy spoke up. "We won't be able to see them, from here."

The service took 20 minutes. The crowd sang the school song at the end.

Everyone celebrated Hank's life with a cheer from the crowd. A reception took place in the fellowship hall where the Engleman family attended church. The band played a few songs, including a jazz piece that Hank loved. The cheerleaders dedicated a special cheer to Hank.

"What an awesome way to celebrate," Christy spoke up to Julie as they sat with plates of food. They ate at a table with two sets of parents from the high school.

Julie introduced herself and then Christy. She explained that Aaron never did say exactly what his parents did, except that they were educators. Now she knew, Aaron's dad was a high school principal of a big high school in Helena. Hank wanted a fun and happy celebration of his life. From what the parents said he was a fair, firm, conscientious man who had been the principal for 20 years. More than that, he was loved, by almost everyone.

"I found you."

She heard the familiar voice and looked around. Julie stood and moved from the table. She opened her arms to Aaron, and they hugged for a long time.

"Thank you for coming, Julie," he whispered in her ear.

"It was the right thing to do, Aaron."

They let go of each other, and Aaron hugged Christy as she stood. He acknowledged the two sets of parents at the table.

After they exchanged names, one dad spoke up, "Aaron, your dad, wow, he really loved kids."

Julie saw the other three parents nod their heads in agreement.

"Thank you everyone for coming," Aaron stammered; he felt like he was about to lose it.

"Ladies, I want to take you to meet mom."

He calmed down as they walked across the fellowship hall to wait to talk to Aaron's mom.

"Christy and Julie, this is my mom, Stacey."

They exchanged greetings and sympathies.

Julie felt a bit of a shock at seeing Aaron's mom. She looked years younger than her age. Julie figured it was because of working with kids, or genetics, or both. Stacey had the same brown eyes as Aaron, but her hair was a little lighter color. Julie remembered the picture at the entrance of the fellowship hall of Aaron's dad. Aaron picked up parts of both his parents, but he definitely had his dad's wide smile.

"I would like to see you tonight, Julie. You and Christy, headed back tomorrow?"

"Uh huh, works busy for both of us."

"Thank you for meeting me, Julie," Aaron smiled to her as they sat in the little hotel bar. It was the only place open in the hotel facility. "Mom's still with family at home. And gosh, I am so sorry you didn't get a chance to meet my sister. She had so much visiting to do, with some of her high school teachers who still work at dad's high school, and friends who came back for the funeral."

"Aaron," she looked into his eyes as they sat with their glasses of wine, "that was the most awesome celebration of life I've ever been to. Your dad, he must'a been special."

"Yeah, he sure loved kids, gave his whole life, first as elementary, then high school, then coaching, then administration, worked his way up from Dean of Students to Principal."

"I appreciate you meeting me, Julie." His brown eyes sparked into hers. "I want to be with you again, to date, to have fun, each day is precious. As I think of that, I know what I want, and it's you in my life. Yeah, I was a spoiled brat about your helping out your friend. I am sorry for my actions. No excuses, dad's situation worked on me, and my thinking got all messed up."

Julie felt tears glob her eyes; all she could do was nod her head as her tummy continued to flip flop. She remained silent.

"I gotta stay on for the lawyer's reading of dad's will in two days. Mom says she'll do nothing right now about our home, even though it's pretty big. She intends to go back to her students next fall, for sure. She's got to get at least 10 more years in, to have a decent retirement."

"Does she have a support group?"

"Yup, right at the church they attend. I'm surprised at the number of men dad's age who've died in our community."

Julie looked into Aaron's eyes, "Same thing at home, my granddad, in his late 50's and Mr. McCasland, 60's. Life works men harder; I don't think the women are necessarily tougher."

Julie finished her wine.

"I've got to get to bed. Christy and I plan to leave at daybreak, a long haul back. I'm happy I came."

"So am I."

They stood together.

"Walk you back to your room?"

Julie shook her head, "I want us to part here; it's best. When things settle down back at your practice, please call me."

They hugged, there in the quiet, nearly empty bar.

Julie turned away from him, then turned back, "One day at a time."

Aaron nodded to her, "Yes, one day at a time."

℅

"It'll be a quiet Christmas in the Idaho snow," Julie sang as she finished her shift in Surgery. She and her grandma planned their Christmas much as they had the year before, quiet because Julie pulled a 10 day straight shift to help out over the holidays. Julie felt a lot stronger with her nursing skills. Surgery lost one nurse to a maternity leave that would extend on into the spring. Everyone tightened their belts to work harder. No one would be brought in to replace her. Hospital administration expected the nurse to return.

Aaron and Julie planned a date for once every week, but that often did not work out. Aaron's reputation spread far away from Twin Trails. He knew he would have to make a decision about the boundaries of his veterinary practice before long. He felt exhausted, stressed out from so much vet work away from the office.

Aaron and Julie continued to be more and more comfortable together, still learning lots of history about each other. Julie finally shared more of her life as a young person in Empireville, prior to her leaving for Montana.

"Our lives, at least mine, stuff just keeps getting better and better, for me," Julie told him that a week before Christmas.

They hugged and let go of each other after they cleaned up from the meal they just ate.

"Can't really make plans, working so many days in a row."

"We'll manage, Julie, each time we're together."

She nodded and finished, "is precious."

℃

"Julie, sorry to wake you, it's your grandma; we've got her in ER, in by ambulance."

"Tell me, Brian."

"I'm the charge nurse on shift; sounds like she called in her own 911. She's got a lot of pain, cold she can't shake, cough."

"On my way."

Julie looked at her bedside clock, 1:30 a.m. She tried to recall, but couldn't remember how many days since she and her grandma chatted. Julie was in the middle of her 10 day straight Christmas shift.

"Oh my gosh, Grandma Natalie, I've been neglecting you."

Julie felt the tears down her cheeks as she backed out and headed for the hospital. She shook her head as she recalled how wrapped up she became with her patients, trying to get them healed up and headed home for the holidays.

"Moving her up to medical right now, Julie," the charge nurse spoke up. Julie got a chance to look at the information as soon as staff got her stabilized in her room. Natalie had her eyes closed; the morphine helped with the pain.

"We'll do tests, but think it's her gall bladder; it may need to come out," the attending physician said.

Julie thought to herself, "Yeah, my grandma, maybe in my surgical unit, at least I can keep an eye on her."

For the next three days and nights Julie moved in a fog of work, looking over her grandma, and finishing up a project with her grandma's church group. They worked on it since before Halloween. Natalie shared with Julie how thankful she was that Julie helped the group out.

On the third night Julie went home, ate, and changed into jeans and a sweatshirt. She returned to surgical. After she peeked into her grandma's room, she saw the mess all over the floor. The bed was gone. Julie hurried to the nurses' station, wondering how everything could change so fast, with her grandma's condition.

The charge nurse handed her a note with ICU scrawled on it.

Aaron and Julie walked down the ICU halls, hand in hand.

"Thanks for coming, Aaron."

"I'm here for you; Natalie's in God's hands."

A few minutes later they stood, watching Flight for Life put Natalie in the helicopter.

"Boise's got the best, in the whole state, if anybody can help grandma stay with us, they can there."

Julie heard that from several of the ICU docs and nurses. Her grandma developed a strep pneumonia from the cold she could not shake. So far none of the antibiotics they tried helped. The good news came when Julie learned Natalie's gall bladder removal was successful. So far no infection showed up in the wound or internally.

"We'll manage somehow, Julie, if you feel you need to go to Boise," the charge nurse spoke to her in an assuring voice. At the surgery nurses' station Aaron stood by her as she shook her head.

"Dad's headed for Boise; he'll represent the family and that's good 'cause he hasn't been a part of grandma's life for a long time. You guys here in surgical are so short staffed already. I'm needed here."

She touched her supervisor's arm, "This," she emphasized the word this, "is where I belong. God's in charge, in his hands."

"Thank you, Julie, we'll all breathe a sigh of relief 'cause we have so many surgeries scheduled after Christmas by end year. Unbelievable how people wait until the last minute to schedule planned surgeries," she shook her head to them.

"It's getting later, and you gotta be back here at work before long, wanta getting something in the dining area?"

"Yeah, let's, then I can go home. Grandma and I had Christmas night plans. Would you like to come over for Christmas dinner; I know she'd want you to be there for me?"

"Absolutely, my schedule is clear for Christmas Day. We'll be busy at the clinic the next day."

They hugged in the employee parking lot. Aaron left her and found his car in public parking. He started to tear up once he got headed for his apartment.

He spoke out, "Losing dad affected me more than I ever could've imagined. Julie stood by me these past months, from June to now, as I picked my life back up. Now I gotta back her up. Her work is hard, physically and mentally. She takes care of me. I gotta take care of her."

He wiped the tears from his cheeks as he nodded his head with his resolve.

ℂ

Julie checked her grandma's place nearly every day on the way home from work, picking up her mail and making sure the pretty tree in the living room had water. Julie kept the presents under the tree, for the day Natalie would be well enough to come back to her own home. She started to bring items from the refrigerator that would spoil to her own home. One of the neighbors agreed to shovel all the sidewalks and driveway for the next month. Julie insisted on paying him.

Folks crowded into midnight mass. Julie felt so proud; she received communion for the first time.

"Thank you God, for your gift of the bread," she thought as she knelt after receiving the bread.

Aaron took her hand and squeezed it gently. They smiled to each other.

The spectacle of the lit candles in the darkened church brought goosebumps to Julie's arms and back. She felt hot tears as the congregation sang *Silent Night.*

As they held hands walking to his truck he asked, "Happy?"

She turned to him, "So happy."

At the truck they hugged and whispered "Merry Christmas" to each other.

℺

"Thank you, Julie and Aaron, for making sure I got well," Natalie smiled to them.

"No way, Grandma, you did that yourself. We just kinda nudged you along the way. They figured out what worked for your pneumonia. You gave Dad a good scare."

"Yeah, a rough 24 hours I don't remember. After that I went from ICU to medical in Boise. Now here I am. It's the 15th of January; I guess I lost nearly a month."

"You did, but it's time to celebrate Christmas. I made wassail and brought it for the meal. You baked the ham, and Aaron contributed scalloped potatoes."

"Uh, sure hoping, you remembered."

Aaron got cut off by Julie.

"Uh huh, the chocolate chip bars, oh yes I did, a Christmas with no dessert, not possible."

The three of them laughed as they dug into the meal.

"I think I'll need home health care for maybe three more days, then I'll be on my own."

"Right Grandma, that's what the docs think."

"And us too," Aaron agreed.

$$8$$

Aaron moved into Julie's home at Halloween the next fall.

"We really are just down the lane from each other now," they laughed as they shared with friends and family.

Julie marveled at how few personal possessions Aaron had.

"I've lived a Spartan existence, getting the student loans paid off," he told her as she helped him move. "I think I shared that with you when we first knew each other."

He watched her nod to him.

At Thanksgiving they found ring sets, one that Aaron liked and fit his finger, and engagement and wedding rings that Julie wanted.

She told him before that, "Let me pick out my own ring and have it sized. You do the same thing."

"Hey, you know I'll not be wearing my ring on duty, with surgeries and such."

"I understand, and I love you for seeing the practical, not so romantic side of me about the rings."

One Sunday morning after Thanksgiving they spooned together before getting up for Sunday church.

"Julie," he whispered into her ear, "Marry me, between Christmas and New Year's. What'cha think?"

She turned to him.

Their brown eyes fired into each other's.

"Wow," she paused, unable to speak. "That, that's so exciting, my best Christmas present, a husband."

They turned into each other laughing, "A wife."

They stopped, kissing and kissing.

"Somethin' simple, just your Grandma, my mom, and your parents."

"Outstanding, you'll help with the planning, Aaron?"

"Course, you always gotta work straight through over the holidays, maybe they'll give you a day off to get married?"

They laughed together, "I sure hope so," was Julie's reply.

ℴℴ

Julie heard the snow falling on the roof of the hospital chapel. She watched the two candle flames flicker and dance at the tiny altar in the center of the circular room. Aaron gazed around at their smiling families, seated for the wedding ceremony.

Later they held hands when they were not greeting guests.

"It was an awesome ceremony, our vows, our folks with us."

"Perfect," Julie whispered to him.

They planned a tiny family wedding, but lots of guests were invited to the reception at their home several hours later. Fellow hospital workers and some of Aaron's clients along with children from Julie's reading group stopped by with their parents.

Julie gazed around at all the guests, eating and chatting. She admired the shimmering Christmas tree with its gold and silver bulbs and banners streaming down.

"So much life here, happiness, and joy, it's so grand," Julie whispered as she stood alone for a moment.

She joined Aaron as they stood near the wedding cake.

"You were off somewhere, over by the tree, Julie."

"Uh huh, thinking about you, about me, our love, Aaron."

He kissed her, "Our love."

SKY TOSSED

15-year-old Hayley copes with the loss of her mom as well as the pressures of her high school studies. Brent becomes her friend, takes her flying and mentors her. They come to care a great deal for each other. Hayley also attends night school at a community college to earn her welding certification. With Brent's encouragement she decides to study nursing and apply for a military scholarship. He goes away to college. His whininess causes Hayley to stop calling him.

Gabe and Hayley work at the same welding shop during the summer. He captures her attention as she completes high school. Brent does the unthinkable. Hayley receives a military scholarship which enables her to begin her nursing program and to join the Air Force ROTC detachment at the University of Iowa. She discovers how me-centric her world is. She vows to change that and becomes friends with an older couple her grandma knew back in Germany. She develops a friendship with Jacob, a fellow nursing student, and romantic relationships with Clay, an ROTC cadet, and Grady.

A few years pass. Hayley completes her BSN and becomes certified as an RN. She loves both Clay and Grady. Life flings Grady into a Peace Corps assignment and Clay into pilot training in Texas. Hayley is assigned to Elmendorf AFB as a 2nd lieutenant. Before moving to her base, she returns home. A surprise, a note and decisions await her.

ABOUT CATHLEEN

www.CathleenEllis.com

Cathleen Ellis is a Colorado native. She and her husband, John, live in the northern part of the state. They have four sons, three daughters-in-law, and four grandchildren. Cathleen draws the inspiration for her love stories from the lives of young people with whom she has lived and worked her entire life.